PRAISE FOR *Follow the Angels, Follow the Doves: The Bass Reeves Trilogy, Book One*

"Thompson's historical novel delivers an unforgettable character based on a true American hero . . . a believable coming-of-age story that echoes *Huckleberry Finn* in its realism and social observation."

—MICHAEL RAY TAYLOR, *The Commercial Appeal*

"Thompson's short novel is a fascinating look at life in northwest Arkansas in the years before and during the Civil War, when the future lawman came of age and ultimately made his break for freedom. The rest of the trilogy is likely to be just as intriguing, especially because that's the way the real Bass Reeves lived his life."

—GLEN SEEBER, *The Oklahoman*

"[Thompson] is a highly entertaining writer, and his Bass Reeves emerges as an intelligent, reluctantly violent, sympathetic young man. Readers will find the compelling recreations of two important Civil War battles to be a kind of bonus."

—JOHN MORT, *The Clarion Ledger*

"Fearless and unflinching, *Follow the Angels, Follow the Doves* is a magnificent work of historical fiction. The characters and the times in which they lived are intensely and beautifully realized, and every line rings with authenticity. . . . Its truths are ever so urgent."

—STEVE YARBROUGH, author of *The Unmade World: A Novel*

"Sidney Thompson has the ability to pull you into the narrative and give you a glimpse of the antebellum life of a young slave destined for greatness as a lawman. . . . Highly recommended."

—ART T. BURTON, author of *Black Gun, Silver Star: The Life and Legend of Frontier Marshal Bass Reeves*

"This novel, like all the best historical fiction, reminds us that the most memorable events in our history happened in specific minutes, hours, and days to individuals every bit as complicated and contradictory as you or me."

—SUSAN PERABO, author of *The Fall of Lisa Bellow: A Novel*

THE BASS REEVES TRILOGY

Book One
Follow the Angels, Follow the Doves

Book Two
Hell on the Border

HELL ON THE BORDER

The Bass Reeves Trilogy, Book Two

SIDNEY THOMPSON

University of Nebraska Press
Lincoln

The epigraph by Aimé Césaire is from
The Original 1939 Notebook of a Return to the Native Land: Bilingual Edition, translation by A. James Arnold and Clayton Eshleman (Middletown CT: Wesleyan University Press, 2013). Earlier versions of chapters "The Coldirons" and "Scrambled Eggs and Brains and Ripe Cantaloupe" (as "Skunk Hour") appeared in *Ginosko Literary Journal*, no. 15 (Fall 2014), and *Prick of the Spindle* 7, no. 3 (Fall 2013), respectively.

Library of Congress Cataloging-in-Publication Data
Names: Thompson, Sidney, 1965– author.
Title: Hell on the border / Sidney Thompson.
Description: Lincoln: University of Nebraska Press, [2021] | Series: The Bass Reeves trilogy; book two
Identifiers: LCCN 2020019506
ISBN 9781496220318 (paperback)
ISBN 9781496225399 (epub)
ISBN 9781496225405 (mobi)
ISBN 9781496225412 (pdf)
Subjects: LCSH: Reeves, Bass. | United States marshals—Indian Territory—Biography. | African Americans—Indian Territory—Biography. | Outlaws—Indian Territory—History—19th century. | Indian Territory—Biography.
Classification: LCC F697.R44 T475 2021 | DDC 363.28/2089960730766 [B]—dc23
LC record available at https://lccn.loc.gov/2020019506

Set in Minion Pro by Mikala R. Kolander.

For Sara
& the young'uns

From looking at trees I have become a tree
and my long tree-feet have dug in the ground
long serpent holes presaging the pillage to come
to high cities of bone.

AIMÉ CÉSAIRE, *Notebook of a Return
to the Native Land*

I bequeath myself to the dirt
   to grow from the grass I love,
If you want me again look
   for me under your boot-soles.

WALT WHITMAN, "Song of Myself"

Contents

Note on Language   xi

PART 1. BEFORE

1. The Coldirons   3

PART 2. DURING

2. Tick Tick   25
3. Tamales   31
4. Twelve   39
5. Scrambled Eggs and Brains
   and Ripe Cantaloupe   43
6. The Dead Line   55
7. There Were Cattle   64
8. Webb Again   70
9. High Horse   82
10. Somewhere at Sea   86
11. Tock Tock   94
12. A Deeper Darkness   103

PART 3. AFTER

13. A Wake   115
14. A Tail   124

15. A Hole   136
16. The Blackness   147
17. A Case   161

Acknowledgments   173

ILLUSTRATIONS

1. Map of Indian Territory
   (Oklahoma), 1883   xiv
2. "Hell on the Border" jail   160

Note on Language

A note about the use of two offensive words. First, the policy of the University of Nebraska Press is not to print n—— because the press "values a thoughtful and ethical use of language." I abhor its casual and slanderous use as well, but my ethical responsibility as a writer of historical fiction is to re-create the past as I honestly see and feel it. Because I want readers to experience the violence, repression, inhumanity, and hate of nineteenth-century America for its teachable lessons, I have chosen to include this word, even if it appears in a compromised manner, as "n——" or "n——s." Neither the press nor I intend to suggest at any time that the characters using the implied epithet are supplying the blanks themselves out of cultural sensitivity. Sensitivity to the contemporary reader is the only concern. Second, I have elected to use the word *squaw* for the purpose of historical verisimilitude. Since "s——," or the s-word, does not yet appear either in any dictionary or in common speech, there is no immediately recognizable substitute to use. Please understand that I am not ignoring the word's offensiveness or intending to perpetuate it.

HELL ON THE
BORDER

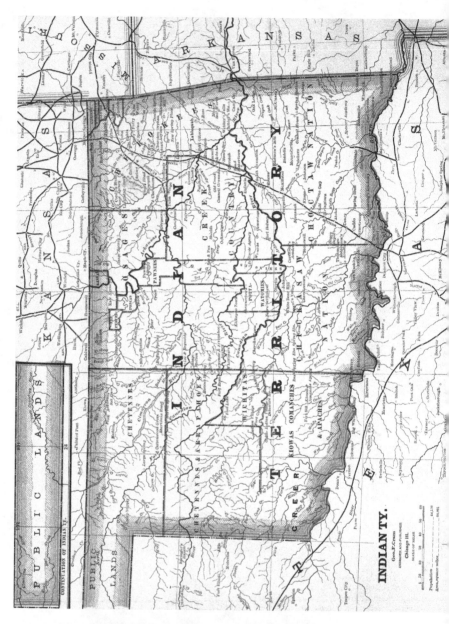

1. Map of Indian Territory (Oklahoma), 1883. Drawn by George Franklin Cram. Published in *Cram's Unrivaled Family Atlas of the World* by A. C. Shewey and Co., Chicago, 1883. David Rumsey Map Collection, www.davidrumsey.com.

PART ONE

BEFORE

1

The Coldirons

To arrest Thomas and Wayne Coldiron in 1883, Bass Reeves had taken off on foot, leaving his small outfit of two men and two wagons behind at their camp on Corn Creek to continue south through the Choctaw Nation, on a rickety cane and in tramp shoes, patched overalls, and a floppy felt hat, for twenty-eight miles, as deep as a lone ranger could get, almost to Texas.

Ruth Coldiron was a widow with a green thumb who lived in a cabin on a parcel of bottomland between Blue River and Island Bayou, and due to these barriers, the homestead was impossible for a posse to reach without giving advanced warning to the few residents of the area, with only a single solid road leading to it. Mrs. Coldiron's cabin was heralded as something of a Hansel and Gretel house of flowers instead of gingerbread. Although she was the mother of two heathen sons, she supposedly lived alone.

Midway between Corn Creek and the Coldiron home, Bass stopped for the night under a cluster of pines in a desolate forest and finished his meager provisions of salt pork and corn dodgers. He stroked his unwieldy mustache, splayed across his face like an old paint brush. Not yet content with his disguise, he twisted the heels off his shoes and drew his Colt, firing three times through the brim and crown of his hat.

The moon was full that night but distant, no bigger round than a .45-caliber entry, as if he'd made it himself.

A full moon usually meant nothing more to Bass than what it was. He preferred to believe he was too Christian to be superstitious. But if the full moon was a distant one, he was sometimes reminded of his

Van Buren home, when he was a slave and happy child, not yet told what he was. Some nights, when his mother and the other slaves in the quarters had fallen asleep, if he knew the moon was full and low enough in the sky, he'd rise from his pallet on the floor and tiptoe past their beds to the front door and pull the plug of sack cloth out of the knothole to scope the moon. He'd then slowly back away and view the moon-filled knothole from the stitched stars of his quilt, and with the stars he could feel beneath his palms and naked legs, and with the moon he could see, it was as if he were outside with the night, and older, and on the prowl for outlaws, as if he were a free and right man. As if he knew his life would come to this.

His mother had buried a stillborn boy and a month-old girl in the shade of a mimosa behind the slave cabin. As soon as Bass had learned to walk, he learned to help her keep the graves of his older siblings tidy. He'd gather up the frail fallen blossoms and fernlike leaves and twigs, and he'd sweep the dirt. Then, as if practicing signing his name, he'd draw crosses in the dirt with his finger. "They spirits is with you, Bass," Pearlalee would tell him. "You remember, you is always more than just one boy." He'd asked once what their names were, and she told him they didn't have names and didn't need them. She smiled and bent to him as if to hug him. "Because," she said and swatted his bottom, "you got yours."

Whenever he thought about his older brother and sister, he thought about what he strove for, and it was for nothing less than to turn back evil more and more and not less and less. To reverse the trends of man and the history of the world, if he could, and to call evil out for what it was, one slave at a time. He saw the slavery or potential slavery in all of them—the thieves, the whiskey peddlers, the rapists, the murderers—and they all needed freeing. Like Jacob in the Bible, Bass could outsmart and outfight whomever he needed and still be a righteous man, or as good as Jacob was good. And if he had to lie and connive and disguise himself as Jacob had done in order to win his father's blessing over his elder brother, Esau, then Bass would do that, too. To catch big-dollar fish like the Coldirons, he would. It was his wish and his living, the grass he grazed, and though he'd get paid if he killed them, either way, he wanted each and every time to save them, to catch them and free their hearts. It was why he'd become a deputy in the first place. Because he believed in freedom.

So he followed in Jacob's footsteps because Jacob proved you didn't have to be that good to be good enough to turn back evil and win God's favor and forge your own nation, even while making a good living and providing for your family—because even though Jacob was bad, he wasn't too bad, and that was the key.

◆ ◆ ◆

At the first sound of birdsong, he rose from his bed of pine needles and continued his trek to Mrs. Coldiron's cabin.

He'd heard Lighthorse police use the Coldiron homestead as a landmark to describe the location of good hunting grounds for boar and deer. Where else would wild boys hide? Two marshals, four deputies, and a dead Pinkerton had failed to catch them there or anywhere else, with the last attempt having come three weeks ago. Floyd Wilson, Bass's posseman, had read the last report aloud to him, which told how the misguided deputy had ridden up to the homestead in the middle of the night, all the way from Atoka, with seven possemen and an Indian scout. The report said that there were no signs of the sons or of any stolen property, and that the mother was clearly ignorant of their whereabouts, having collapsed into tears upon learning of her sons' multiple counts of murder and train robbery.

Late on the second day, Bass passed half a dozen children, Indian mixed with Negro, watching him from a swamp. A skeletal red hound pup wandered out of the weeds to sniff his shoes and followed him close to an hour, until Bass spotted a rat snake; pinning the snake's head with the tip of his cane, he grabbed the tail and swung its head against the ground. The pup danced as Bass peeled the snake's skin from around its mouth and then yanked it all the way off its body as if it were a sock. Once he dropped the rope of meat, the pup stopped following.

Approaching twilight a double colonnade of daffodils, touch-me-nots, and bearded irises beckoned him off the road and onto what must have been the right path. Ahead, azalea bushes and day lilies and more irises bloomed in thick clouds of color around the gray cabin and around the pig pen and outhouse, all pitched in a row on the edge of a wood. In flower boxes hanging below each cabin window grew tall pink and lavender and yellow tulips, like lollipops.

It was no exaggeration of exhaustion when Bass tripped on the front step and stumbled up to the door. Leaning forward on his mud-tipped cane, flat-footed in his mud-caked shoes, he stretched his long arm out and knocked and called hello.

The muslin curtains flickered in the window to his left just before the porch boards rippled beneath him from movement inside, just before the door opened. The woman reminded him of his own mother, with her graying black hair and strong, square frame, faded flowered dress, and thick bare feet. She was as unafraid of him as she could be, waiting patiently for him to speak.

He removed his hat and crushed it to his heart, giving her a humble nod. "Sorry to take you away from your family this evening," he said, "but I'm real hungry, ma'am, and wondering if I could beg a bite to eat, just anything. Don't matter. A hog scrap'll do, ma'am."

She held her forearms across her chest and studied him down to his shoes. "Where you from?"

"Trying to get back to Paris on nothing but a rickety cane and two blistered feet, ma'am. I've come a long way, and I'll be honest, the men of the law's after me. They hard on my trail for a trifle, even shot at me three times, and I mean close ones, see?" He showed her the holes in his hat.

"I'll say," she said.

"Yes, ma'am," he said, setting his hat back on his head. "Now, this is my first stop, so if I'd be putting you out any, I can try elsewhere."

"Nonsense," she said. "You come on inside. I will gladly give you something to eat."

"Yes, ma'am," he said. "Thank you, ma'am." He bent over to unlace his shoes, and the two sets of handcuffs he'd sewn on the underside of his overalls pressed against his ribs. He sucked in his gut to relieve the pressure on the stitches, and he inadvertently gasped.

"Be careful." She reached out to steady him.

"Yes, ma'am. Thank you, ma'am," he said, rising up on his cane. Gingerly, he hulled his feet from his shoes. "That's better."

"Good. Well, come on inside," she said, backing away to let him by. "Just us tonight. You ain't interrupting nothing."

He dropped his left hand near his pocket where his Colt was, and with his cane in his right hand he lowered his head and stepped into a kitchen with a table and four empty chairs. He looked elsewhere, toward the hutch and basin, toward the rocker and knitting stand, then beyond the potbelly stove to two back rooms with doors standing open, showing beds in the rooms. But from what he could see in the scant light from the two front windows, her sons were not here. And there didn't appear to be a rear-entry door for escape. Her sons were slippery to have been seen slipping in and out for months and to have never gotten caught.

"Glad to have the company," she said. She shut the door behind him.

"Yes, ma'am. Me, too. Me, too. Been awhile."

She patted the back of a chair. "Have yourself a seat."

"Thank you," he said. He hung his cane on the back of the chair and sat down. He watched her open a cupboard on the hutch and take out a covered plate. Her feet whisked across the sandy floor.

"Not much, I'm afraid," she said. She set the plate in front of him and pulled away the fabric of an old flour sack to reveal, he couldn't believe his eyes, salt pork and corn dodgers. "But help yourself. I done ate."

"No, this is more than generous." He didn't hesitate to collect a slice of pork and a corn dodger and pop them into his mouth.

"I got some mesquite jelly to help those dodgers go down, if you like mesquite jelly."

He was still chewing, unprepared to speak, so he waved her off.

"Well, you'll need something to make them go down." She returned from the cupboard with a glass and a demijohn hanging on her thumb. "Don't get excited now because this is just water. Don't keep nothing harder."

He shook his head and swallowed. "Much obliged, ma'am." He brushed his hands on his pants legs before reaching for the demijohn. He unstopped the cork and filled his glass. "And, ma'am, I don't want to alarm you if you was to see this here side arm peeking out my pocket." He plugged the cork back in the demijohn and withdrew his Colt, laying it on the table. "You can hold onto it until I go if you like. Up to you."

She smiled with a nod. "I appreciate that."

"I'm Jacob, by the way." He tipped the brim of his hat, and his thumb slipped through one of the bullet holes.

She noticed and snickered. "And I'm Mama," she said. "Everybody calls me Mama."

"Yes, ma'am," he said. "Nice to meet you." He reached for another corn dodger, and Mama reached for his Colt, taking it by the barrel and walking away, into the bedroom on the left. He didn't expect that. Behind her door he heard only her sandy feet start and stop, start and stop.

He drank his glass of water and refilled the glass.

She returned and sat across the table. An unlit oil lamp and a box of matches sat on a doily between them.

He smiled and sandwiched a slice of pork between two corn dodgers.

"You know," she said, "I've got two boys, and they're always wanted by the law, being pursued by the law."

He nodded. "Law's getting tougher and tougher these days."

"I tried to tell my husband this weren't no place to raise them boys, free land or not, but he wouldn't listen." She rested her chin in her hand and looked off toward one of the windows as if from that distance she could see anything more than the light of dusk through the swirls of the handblown glass. "I blame the place more than them boys, though. Boys will be boys, you know?" She cut her eyes at him. "You know, don't you?"

"Unfortunately, ma'am."

She stretched her lips in a taut and level smile. "Glad to help."

"I appreciate it," he said.

"Soon as you're done, we got a creek out back. It'll do you good for them blisters to get a quick dip."

"Yes, ma'am," he said. "I know I must be ripe."

"Well, that, too." She rapped her knuckles on the tabletop, then stepped away.

Bass gave the cabin another once-over, registering the location of, and distance between, doors and possible weapons in case later in the dark he needed a stove log or a knitting needle or to dash from room to room or find his way outside—because he considered it now a good sign Mrs. Coldiron had taken his pistol. Apparently, she was allowing him to stay the night.

When she returned from her bedroom with a bath towel and a half-melted bar of lye, he'd cleared his plate and was brushing crumbs out of his mustache.

"Here," she said, handing him the soap and draping the towel over his arm. "Take the path by the outhouse. Straight back."

He smiled, reached for his cane, and slowly stood up. "Thank you, ma'am—I mean, *Mama*."

"That's right," she said. She reached for the matches. "Better hurry."

The path by the outhouse led him through mesquite, cedars, and cypress to a sand bank freshly marked by horses. He lowered to his haunches. There were two sets, one shod and one not. Upstream and down, the creek widened and darkened, but the passage for a horse here at the bend would be an easy leap.

He held his breath and listened for hoof stamps or whinnies and blows from horses maybe tied to a tree somewhere out of sight.

When he heard nothing but a breeze rattling the high boughs and, closer, a trickle of water dripping from the wings of a goldfinch, he decided to relax and undress and jump in.

Of course, his dip would be quick. This water was as cold as Corn Creek. He froze going under, even as he thrashed—his heart and mind and nerves all wired up and electric as Thomas Edison's famous bulb.

He hung the towel over the porch rail to dry and set the soap on the rail beside it, then opened the cabin door. "Woo," he said, shivering, back in his undershirt and overalls and bullet-holed hat but still cold.

"Feel better?" She was rocking in her rocker and knitting in the lamp light.

He laughed and shut the door. "I'll tell you in the morning."

"Well, good, I was hoping you'd know you was welcome to stay the night. People is people with me."

"God bless you, ma'am."

She angled her head toward the bedroom on the right. An oil lamp dimly flickered in it. "I done fixed up my boys' room for you, so make yourself at home, Jacob. Get some rest. And I'll make sure to see you off in the morning with something a might better than leftover corn dodgers." She chuckled with her eyes closed, and like his mother, her whole body jiggled.

"Yes, ma'am. Thank you, ma'am," he said, nodding. He removed his hat. "You mighty kind, mighty kind." He approached her, still nodding. "I got ten young'uns, five boys and five girls, and the most beautiful wife. I'm blessed, truly blessed. I just wanna get home to them."

"Well, they need you more than you can know. It's going on four years since my husband passed and we weren't all that close, kind of like strangers really, but still every day it's hard to believe he ain't anymore with me."

"Yes, ma'am," he said. "And Indian Territory, like you say, it ain't the best place to be raising boys, *or* girls for that matter. Too much freedom can become too much slavery if you can believe that."

"Mmhmm," she said.

"But the same goes for a place like Paris, being so close by. What's in your backyard gets tracked in the house, am I wrong?"

"No, you're right," she said, her knitting needles clicking like a telegraph.

"I grew up with no freedom and done wandered long enough across Indian Territory, and I can tell you both ways is no good. I keep praying one day I'll find myself on a middle ground."

She stopped rocking and collapsed her hands around her needles and yarn. "I'll pray tonight for you and your family."

"And I'll return the favor."

She smiled and started her rocker, continuing to work her needles.

He clasped the bedroom door behind him, and on the table beside the lamp he found a vase of three freshly clipped tulips, each of a different color. He lowered his nose to breathe their sweet scent, undressed to his underwear, and climbed into Thomas and Wayne Coldiron's bed. If they didn't show by morning, he would pretend to leave and stake out the creek instead.

He snuffed out the wick and prayed that he would have the opportunity to teach Thomas and Wayne right from wrong and to find Jesus, and that he wouldn't have to kill them. But if he did have to, that he wouldn't have to in front of their mother.

He prayed, too, for his own sons and daughters, who were growing up too quickly during his long and many absences as a deputy. He prayed that they would never stray from Jesus the way the Coldirons had. That they would find that middle ground, if they hadn't found it yet, and that they would hide there—*hide*—and hold on.

◆ ◆ ◆

A sharp but muted whistle deep from within the woods cleaved him from his sleep, though apparently he hadn't been asleep long, waking with full clarity and lifting his head from the feather pillow to hear Mrs. Coldiron's rocker rocking emptily. The cabin jostled as the soft pad of her weight drifted away, across the front room to the front door.

Holding his breath, he heard the wood-on-wood slide of the brace board, then the front door open, making the bedroom door knock on its latch. On the porch Mrs. Coldiron whistled an answer, high in the palate, and immediately came the rumble of horse hooves.

Bass rolled out of bed onto nimble feet and pulled on his overalls as the horses neared. When the horses halted in a scramble out front, he unlocked his door, letting it swing wide. He leaned on his cane in the doorway, as if he were afraid to leave the safety of the room, and listened to their murmured voices. He didn't want to appear as relaxed as he was.

The murmurs continued back and forth outside, and then there was silence. Then a horse nickered. Then bootheels struck the porch. A young man, and another one behind him, walked through the open door, matching the description of Wayne and Thomas—two white men of medium build and dark hair in their twenties.

The first one, who was mustached and carrying a side-by-side Remington shotgun by its grip, strode up to Bass and stopped three feet from him. He didn't aim the barrels at Bass and the hammers weren't cocked, but his fingers rested on both triggers.

"So, n——, who are you?"

"What did I just say to y'all outside?" Mrs. Coldiron asked. "Be nice, Wayne—both of you!"

Bass sized up the other one, the younger one, Thomas, with sideburns to his jawline and a Winchester rifle held across his chest. Both brothers wore pistols tucked in the waistband of their jeans.

"Jacob Jackson," Bass said. That was his pastor's name, and it wasn't the first time Bass had used it.

"Yeah, but why you running?" Wayne asked.

"For introducing spirits," Bass said.

"That's it?" Thomas said. Outside of his sideburns, the only hair on his face was a mangy splotch of fuzz on his chin.

Bass nodded. "That and for shooting my way free, I suppose. So when I heard y'all's horses, I just knowed the law had done found me."

"And they come close to getting you, we hear," Wayne said.

Bass nodded again. "I hear the law's after y'all, too."

The brothers looked at one another, then at their mother.

"I'm sure glad we can join forces for the night," Bass said. "Safer in numbers, you know."

Wayne grunted. "Mama trusts you for some reason."

"Well, she a good woman," Bass said. "Anybody can see that. But if I in the way now, I can go."

"No, you won't!" Mrs. Coldiron said.

Bass stood straight on his cane. "No hard feelings, really, ma'am," he said.

"I said *no*," she said. "We ain't putting you out at this time of night. My boys know how to sleep on the floor." She shuffled toward her bedroom. "I'll get some blankets."

Wayne shrugged. "Floor'll be nicer than where we been sleeping."

Thomas laughed. "That's for damn sure. A bed'll spoil you. Let it spoil you, old man. I don't want it."

Mrs. Coldiron returned with an armful of blankets, left again, and came back with pillows. Then she left again. By this time, Wayne and Thomas had moved Mrs. Coldiron's rocker to the kitchen, spread their blankets on the floor, and taken off their boots and coats and were lying in their clothes with their guns beside them, passing a bottle of whiskey. Bass was taking his turn having a snort when Mrs. Coldiron came out of her bedroom carrying his Colt six-shooter out in front of her by the nose of the barrel as though she were toting a dead rat.

"I reckon with my boys home you can have this back now," she said. "Just watch after them's all I ask. I know they'll do the same."

"Yes, ma'am," Bass said. "I owe that to you and more." He handed the whiskey to Thomas and reached for his Colt, but Thomas reached faster, lunging past him with the whiskey and snatching the Colt from his mother's fingertips.

"Thomas!" Mrs. Coldiron scolded in a high pitch. "Don't be a child, boy. Give the man his gun."

Thomas fell back on his blanket and dropped the Colt beside his own guns. "When need be or if be," he said and plugged the bottle to his lips.

Bass watched the bubbles rumble. "Quite all right, ma'am," he said. "He don't know me yet. He will."

Mrs. Coldiron turned to her son Wayne and stooped to pat the top of his head. "Y'all been getting along, not fighting again, have you?"

"I only needed to embarrass him once, Mama," Thomas said.

"Shit," Wayne said.

"Uh-huh," Thomas said. He took a second swig from the bottle before passing it to his brother.

Mrs. Coldiron held her forearms across her chest, eyeing Thomas. "Who else you got to rely on out there but each other?" When he didn't answer, only picked at a loose thread on his blanket, she spoke louder. "Listening to me?" she said.

Still not answering, ignoring her, Thomas ran the thread between his upper front teeth.

"You know," Bass said, "I always say, 'You choose your friends, but the Good Lord chooses your family.' You know, who you gonna trust more—*your* judgment or the *Good Lord's*?" He smiled, but only Mrs. Coldiron appeared to pay him any attention. Wayne was pulling off his socks. Thomas was still working the thread through his teeth. "That's what I tell my young'uns when they start to get cross with each other. Makes you think."

"Sure does, don't it, boys?"

"Course," Thomas said, lowering the thread and pausing to swallow, "the Good Lord didn't mind crossing His only begotten son, did He?"

Mrs. Coldiron consulted Bass. "See what I'm talking about? What I'm dealing with here?"

"Yes, ma'am," Bass chuckled.

Thomas reached for Bass's Colt. "What if I was to take up a gun, any old gun, like so and aim it like so," he said, aiming it at his mother and drawing back the hammer, "and if I was to fire a ball of lead smack between my mama's eyes out of some kind of sacrifice for humanity? Would you bow down to me then, Mr. Old Christian Man? Would you say Heaven was in my eyes and the Holy Ghost was in my heart?"

"Hush your mouth and set Mr. Jacob's gun down this instant, boy!" Mrs. Coldiron said.

"All for the same humanity, by the way," Thomas said, "whose judgment we can't trust in the first place. That make sense to you?"

"Thomas Lee!" Mrs. Coldiron said.

Wayne threw his socks at Thomas and laughed. "Enough already."

Thomas eased the hammer down and tossed the Colt back on his blanket. "Just a point."

Mrs. Coldiron wagged her head, keeping it down.

Wayne gestured to Bass with the bottle, but only a slosh was left, so Bass politely waved it off.

"Go on," Wayne said, pumping the bottle at him. "We got another."

"Much obliged to you," Bass nodded. He took the bottle by its neck, gave the whiskey a swirl, and drained his swallow slowly, thinking things through. His best chance of getting his Colt back and arresting the Coldirons without bloodshed was to corral them, yet very soon he'd be expected to go back to bed. He wiped his mouth and watched Thomas bite down on the cork of a new bottle. It would've been a lot easier for Bass if he'd reached for his Colt as fast as he could've and fired away if the brothers had budged, spilling out their bright young blood before their mother's eyes if he had to. That didn't seem the most Christian way of going about making or keeping peace, or the most logical way to prove Negroes could be trusted with guns and a badge and freedom.

"Well," Mrs. Coldiron said. She took a deep breath and gave Bass a look that seemed to say, *Help me.*

Bass shrugged and handed her the empty bottle. "I hate to go in there to sleep," he said, "and shut this here door."

Wayne's and then Thomas's eyes rolled upward and froze on Bass.

"What if somebody or even a whole bunch of somebodies was to crawl up and try to try something? Being separated in different rooms, we couldn't be much protection to each another. Well, I suppose I be protected a ways more, seeing as y'all out here and taking first what come, but I won't be no protection for y'all or later for me, for that matter." He looked at Mrs. Coldiron, her worried eyes. "Not in the back with nothing, you know?"

"What you getting at?" Wayne asked.

Bass lifted the tip of his cane and pointed at their pallets. "If y'all gonna insist on sleeping on the floor, why not on the bedroom floor with me? That's my thinking. I just wanna get home like y'all done. But if deputies come busting through that front door, you won't have much of a chance to reach, and I won't have *no* chance. Back there, though, we all got a fighting one. You can toss me my Colt when need be, am I right? What y'all think?"

"You want to know what I think?" Thomas said. He tipped the bottle up, gulped, belched, then passed the bottle to Wayne. "I think what I think," he said, "is you need to settle down, Negro. I think what I'm thinking is we're perfectly situated right where we are."

Mrs. Coldiron scratched her arms and tiptoed closer to her sons. "I really would sleep better knowing y'all was together, too."

"Mama?" Wayne said.

"Please, boys," Mrs. Coldiron said.

"Ah, hell," Wayne said. He took a drink and handed the bottle to Bass. "I just want to get some sleep," he said, pushing himself to his feet.

"Jesus, nobody's coming tonight or we'd heard," Thomas said, not moving, except for lolling his head back with his eyes closed.

Bass turned and took a swig as he entered the darkness of the brothers' room. He rested the bottle on the bedside table and fumbled for a matchstick, praying Thomas would change his mind.

"Don't be difficult," Mrs. Coldiron said in the other room. "I just want what's best for you."

The lamp glowed, and Wayne walked in carrying a tangle of guns, a pillow, and a blanket.

"Tommy, please, for tonight," Mrs. Coldiron said.

"Goddammit, Mama," Thomas said in the other room, "you want me to take that bottle from you and break it in your mouth? Goddammit, I will!"

A scuffle commenced and the empty whiskey bottle Bass had given Mrs. Coldiron skittered across the floor. The floor vibrated, making the flames in the lamp dance over the bedroom walls, then after a clatter of gun steel, Thomas stomped into the bedroom with nothing in his arms but his weapons. Mrs. Coldiron shuffled in closely behind him with his blanket and pillow.

"Here you go, Tommy," she said, spreading the blanket carefully on the floor. "You'll feel better after you get some rest. You're just not sleeping enough, son."

With the space on the floor evaporating, Wayne at the foot of the bed and now Thomas between the bed and door, Bass climbed into bed and stretched out above the covers, still in his overalls, keeping his handcuffs close.

"If I hear something funny," Mrs. Coldiron said, "I'll knock on the wall."

"Yes'm," Wayne said.

"Well," she said with a glance to each of them, though Thomas was lying facedown and not seeing her, "good night, boys."

"Good night, ma'am," Bass said.

"Night, Mama," Wayne said, rising again to his feet. He swept the door behind her and dropped the hook in the eye latch.

Bass reached for the wick wheel on the lamp, and once Wayne had raked the whiskey off the table and squatted back down on his pallet, Bass smothered the light.

He wriggled his body as though he were nestling for sleep but was actually positioning himself closer to the edge. When there was silence, it was broken only by an occasional slosh of whiskey or a swallow. The brothers passed their bottle back and forth between them, as if Bass were no longer in the room or they believed him to be asleep.

"Like old times, ain't it?" Wayne said, speaking softly.

Thomas groaned in agreement.

"Was like camping out in our own room," Wayne said.

"At first, maybe," Thomas said. "Then we realized he was putting us out of our damn bed forever."

"Because Mama put him out," Wayne said.

"Yeah, but a *man* would've taken the floor sometimes."

"True," Wayne said.

"Course, we know Daddy weren't no man, or Mama would've been the one in here with us."

"Yeah," Wayne said. "That's true, too."

At some vague point it became clear to Bass that they had stopped talking and wouldn't start up again. From that point on, Bass lay quietly between his own delayed breaths, listening to theirs, which would fade sometimes and he'd believe they were waiting, postponing sleep, too. Their breathing would deepen and lengthen momentarily, and one brother would begin to snore but then would wake himself, and then the other would start and stop.

To guard against sleep and to mark time, Bass recounted what he knew of his ten children. He began with the oldest. Like her daddy, Sallie's favorite color was red. Red licorice, red bows, red barns, red roses, red horses. Bass remembered teaching her the word *Oklahoma*, Choctaw for "red people."

Bass had noticed that Thomas and Wayne had been asleep nonstop since he recalled the birth of Bennie, his sixth, so when he reached the end of what he knew of Homer, he confidently unfastened the bib of his overalls and began breaking the stitches on the handcuffs. His deputy marshal badge was pinned on the underside of the bib as well, so when the handcuffs were free, he refastened one side of the bib but not both, wanting the badge side to fold down and show them who he was.

He stretched a leg over the edge of the bed. Once his toes touched the floor, he rolled his weight off the bed and onto his foot and stood without a sound that either of those boys would hear. The small curtained window provided very little light, but enough for him to make out the arms and hands of white men.

In slow, small steps he neared the foot of the bed and bent down without hesitation, scooping a bracelet around Wayne's wrist and clicking it locked—ready to reach for Wayne's glinting pistol if they roused, but neither roused. That was the easier hand, though. Wayne was lying on his back with his hands at his sides, so Bass would have to carry the cuffed hand across his body in order to chain it to the other.

For better balance and defensive posture, Bass straddled himself over Wayne with his feet firmly planted away from the blanket on the wood floor, ready to drop down on Wayne's chest and pin his arms with his knees, if need be. He took a deep breath and held it, so his own breathing wouldn't cover the sounds of theirs, then lifted Wayne's hand. It was the dead limb of a child. No resistance, no manhood to Wayne's nerves whatsoever. The second iron click didn't even rouse Thomas.

He collected Wayne's shotgun and pistol and set them on the bed. He crept next toward Thomas, searching out the open floor with his feet before putting his feet down. A floorboard creaked, but again no one stirred. Thomas was even asleep on his stomach with his elbows forked out, his wrists perfectly exposed side by side on his pillow. The Good Lord was answering prayers early this morning.

As before with Wayne, Bass straddled himself over Thomas, and holding his breath he leaned down unceremoniously and locked the handcuffs on him in rapid succession. Of course, no one heard that either. All there was for Bass to do now before his long trek back to camp was catch a little shut-eye, too, it being too early and dark yet to travel.

He plucked up his Colt and slipped it into his pocket, then collected Thomas's rifle and pistol and hid them with Wayne's under the covers before crawling back in bed beside them. He took in and let out his first good breath since leaving the bed minutes earlier and thanked God for it. Everything since arriving at the Coldiron home had gone as easily for him as he'd fathomed—a sign of God's blessing. Blessings had been mounting his entire life.

◆ ◆ ◆

Bass woke revived hours later to a blue dawn and sat up to find Thomas and Wayne still asleep in the same position. He grabbed his cane and hat and stood to the floor.

The young fools. He drew his six-shooter and kicked Wayne in the ribs, then Thomas in the leg. "Come on, boys, let's get going from here." He flicked the latch on the door and watched them in their confused half-sleep try to use their arms and groan and reach for absent guns.

"Y'all under arrest is what's going on," Bass said. "Got your subpoenas at camp. They'll be read to you when we get there. Come on." He stepped through the open door and rapped it with his cane. "Hurry up, now."

Thomas charged headlong at Bass, but Bass buffaloed him in the cheek, and Thomas dropped to his knees.

Bass looked at Wayne, crouched in a stance to run at Bass, too. "Step up, son," he said. "Druther not beat the devil outta you both before you even get awake good, but damn if I won't."

"You'll have to," Wayne said, charging him, and Bass cracked him across the face, too.

"Boys?" The word went up frightfully behind Mrs. Coldiron's closed door.

"Mama!" Wayne called and banged his fist on the wall.

Thomas steadily cursed as he wobbled to his feet. Blood trickled from a cut across his cheek that was nearly identical to the one beginning to open across Wayne's cheek.

"Mama!" Wayne called.

"Don't forget y'all's boots," Bass said.

Thomas walked out first, still steadily cursing him.

Mrs. Coldiron's door flung open and she rushed out in her nightgown, her hands open and flailing, her fingers spread, no steel in them. "What's happening?" she said. "Where y'all going?"

Bass waved his Colt so she could see it. "I'm taking them in, ma'am, so step back."

"You're the law?" she said. "You're the law?"

"Yes, ma'am." He clinked his badge with the nose of his Colt. "Deputy Bass Reeves, and I'm taking them in."

"You that n—— deputy!" Thomas said. "You shitting me! *You?*"

"You're the law?" Mrs. Coldiron asked, too stunned to raise her voice. "You come into my home and you're the law?"

"Damn you!" Wayne grunted. He charged again, and Thomas joined in a half-jump later. Bass struck them back down, one after the other, and Mrs. Coldiron let out a scream.

"I do appreciate everything, ma'am," Bass told her. "I really do."
He turned to her sons, struggling on all fours to stand back up and
bleeding across their faces. "Hurry now and get your boots on. We
got ourselves a long walk ahead."

Her sons finally did as they were told, while Mrs. Coldiron wailed
and stomped her feet.

Bass unlocked the front door and opened it wide to yellowing
light, to the tied horses snorting at the rail. He stood on the porch
putting on his shoes as Thomas and Wayne came out behind him,
followed by their mother.

"We ain't really fucking walking with two good horses right here?"
Thomas said.

"Yep," Bass said, "so we better get a move on quick."

"That's goddamned ridiculous," Thomas said. "How far?"

"You're an evil man," Mrs. Coldiron said.

Bass turned away from Thomas. "Sorry you feel that way, ma'am."
He turned back to Thomas. "Look, I ain't stealing your stolen horses
unless to carry your corpses back. You might rather walk like I'm
doing." He gestured with the Colt for the brothers to walk ahead;
he would follow.

"You're a pig-slopping n—— motherfucker!" Mrs. Coldiron
screamed. "A real dirty whore of a n—— devil motherfucker! You
know that? That's what you are!"

Bass thought when he stopped at the edge of Mrs. Coldiron's
property to pluck one of her red touch-me-nots to slide under
his badge that he'd find her dropping back. But she screamed ever
louder and continued off her path and up the road after them. For
three miles she harassed him.

There was no scent to a touch-me-not, but it was a beautiful,
delicate thing.

PART TWO

DURING

2

Tick Tick

Bass stood before the open chifforobe and straightened his plaid bowtie in the mirror's brown-grained glass. From the chipped porcelain saucer on the shelf, he collected his tin star and pinned it to his houndstooth coat. He inspected its level; then, as one last gesture of decorum, he plucked his tortoise-shell comb up by its mousetail handle and attempted to tidy his mustache. He'd trained his eyes not to glance up because the face he'd see floating there wouldn't closely enough be his. This glass forever robbed the freckles from his cheeks, and his skin appeared much browner than was true.

All but Bass was hushed this morning in anticipation of his exit and undetermined absence in the territory. Outside, even the youngest of his ten children had stopped laughing and squealing at their game of knucklebones on the packed earth beneath the mimosa tree. The only sounds of disregard were the sounds on him, the clinking of cartridges and guns against guns as he stepped away from the chifforobe to walk the hall.

His steps fell into the rhythm of the longcase clock ahead of him in the parlor, though he imagined it as a widecase clock, as wide as the future, whose pendulum swung only forward, like it was walking, so it would eventually leave the showplace with him, swinging and shooing away the past—and the present, too, if the present was the sort of present a body could shake loose from like a cloud of flies on the road.

He never felt more at home than when he did these final steps leaving it.

Jennie waited by the front door so beautifully dark in her pink-and-white striped cotton dress. She was darker than the cherry wood of the clock's case, dark rather like the darkest wet tree bark, whatever that was. She held a covered pail in front of her with both hands, and he marveled that she looked more beautiful, maybe, holding that pail.

"Mercy," he said, "I do believe I married the prettiest woman this side of the Dead Line."

She smiled at his old joke. "I'm not the prettiest on the other side, too?"

He shrugged and stood close enough to her that he could feel the steam from the biscuits in the pail rising through the cloth. "Don't notice no women once I cross the Dead Line. All official."

"Uh-huh," she sass-faced him. "So you notice other women on this side, you're telling me?"

He nodded. "Be noticing enough to see you still the prettiest."

Her smile lengthened; then she puckered her lips, and he leaned down and kissed her.

"Please be careful, Bass," she said.

"Don't know any other way," he said.

"I worry about you," she said.

"You don't know any other way," he said, "but I'll be all right."

She opened her eyes at him as if to soak him up, and when they couldn't grow any wider, as if she had suddenly stopped breathing, like a quit wind, her tenderness congealed, slowly as a falling leaf, into a familiar dead mass of worry. "They need you, too," she said, close to a whisper.

Bass reached around her as well as he could while holding his hat and his Winchester. With her pail bumped against his chest, he shut his eyes and prayed aloud for the Good Lord to stand in as a faithful husband and father until his safe return.

His son Robert had already tacked Strawberry, the unshod sorrel gelding that was Bass's preferred horse, which due to its rough coat and hooves and thick-boned structure looked from a distance more like a pony than the court-issued quarter horses all other lawmen rode. Tied in tow to Strawberry was a bay gelding Robert had named Fringe. Robert was standing with them out front when Bass opened the door. Also out front, in the porch rockers, were Bass's mother, Pearlalee, and Auntie Totty, who likely had moved from the rockers on their porch next door to those on Bass's once they saw Robert leave the stable. The other children, including Sallie, who was the oldest and lived with her husband in a house of their own on the other side of Pearlalee and Auntie Totty, began to gather at the base of the porch steps to say goodbye. The five hock-joints Bass had gotten tossed in for free with a package of lamb chops from a butcher in Fort Smith were left scattered in the dirt among blackened blossoms.

The mimosa's sweet green cucumber scent, early for April, reminded Bass that so many desperate spirits called. He had to fight the urge at home at some point every day to get up and walk on out, and at last he didn't have to. He could now heed their call and would soon be at peace.

Pearlalee and Auntie Totty stilled their hand fans only long enough to give Bass a hug.

"Bring me back some grits," Pearlalee said. It was her usual request, even though the Lighthorse police had rewarded him for his work with some of the staples of their tribes only on a few occasions. For capturing the Coldiron brothers last year, he'd returned home with four ten-pound sacks of milled kernel, and she hadn't let him forget it.

"You know I will, Mama," he said. The Coldirons were hanging today and he would be there to see it, but she wouldn't want to know that.

"And a scalp," ten-year-old Bennie said. "Bring me back a scalp, please, Daddy." The day had hardly begun, yet dust already coated him and made mud in the corners of his mouth.

"I'll scalp *you* if you don't hush it," Pearlalee said.

"Daddy ain't a Indian." Robert clutched the hat off his head and slapped his younger brother across the chest with it, and a puff of dust billowed off him.

Bass felt Jennie's mad mother eyes bearing down hard on him, so he looked her way to try to soothe her, but her lips remained clamped shut like so many a dead man's. He turned back to Bennie and lowered. He shook his head. "I appreciate you saying *please*, though, son."

"A head then, a whole head?" Bennie nodded as if he actually believed Bass would agree to it. "Please, please, *please!*"

The youngest of the girls covered their mouths.

"Daddy ain't a outlaw neither," Robert said. "Deputies bring back boots nowadays if they bring back anything."

"But it's always better to bring people in alive," Bass said, patting Bennie on the head. The little lamb. "That's what civilized lawmen do because outlaws are people, too, son. Like you or me. They need to be shown a better way."

"Okay, bring back boots then," Bennie said, "with blood on them."

Bass allowed himself to smile. There had been a time when every dream of his was also about working some violence on bad people. Boys could be that way.

"And some licorice! Please, Daddy," piped Lula, clutching the hem of her dress.

Bass had always made an effort to bring something back for everyone. Sometimes food but sometimes a play-pretty or a piece of pottery or a dog or knife or nice Indian blankets. At the very least a painted fan or magazine.

He kissed his daughters, hugged his younger sons, shook hands with the older ones, then Bass sat in his saddle with the good posture of a cavalry officer. With the bay in tow, he clicked for Strawberry to follow the road that followed the railroad, which wound through town along the Arkansas River, until they reached the ferry crossing. Within a matter of minutes, he was already drifting west, toward dark skies.

Johnny Russom's laughter filled the air. He was the same shirt-less, rail-thin ferryman who'd delivered Bass to the Fort Smith side of the river for all nine years of his service to the law, since 1875. A white man who'd become darker from the sun than Bass was and laughed all day beneath a broad straw hat.

"And then on Wednesday you may've heard, listen to this," Johnny said, already moving into another story, never stopping. Never did. "So I had this horse trader come up with four Appaloosas and try to pay me passage for just him, not the horses, mind you." He squawked a laugh, and though he was telling the story to Bass, he told it loud enough for others on the ferry to hear and constantly surveyed for their attention.

"'The horses know how to swim,' the fellow said," Johnny said. "Ha! 'They know how to drown, too,' I told him, and so he said, 'How much you wanna wager?' How about that for you? So I come back at him, saying, 'I ain't wagering a fool bet like that even if you is the fool.' I mean, I didn't know his horses from Adam. Maybe they could swim the Red Sea with or without Moses, you know?"

"I do," Bass said.

Johnny threw his hands into the air and looked around. "It was up to him to lose them or not if he wanted, right? So I set off with just him, but he whistled, and one by one those Appaloosas followed us into the water. We weren't halfway across when the first of those Appaloosas went under and then all four, bobbing like corks and fighting the current until finally washing up at that bar yonder. See them spots up under them buzzards?" He pointed his arm, black as a bay's mane, and gazed at Bass with no smile in his eyes or in his silence anywhere.

Bass hoped to have a long line of Strawberrys in his life. This one and the first one wouldn't be enough trusted horse.

"Must have stole them horses, don't you reckon, Bass?"

Bass nodded. "Likely."

"Yeah, you might want to keep an eye out for him. A man without a horse." Johnny squawked. "Some people!"

◆ ◆ ◆

This process of leaving home always had the same effect on him. Once he woke and took his first steps, he began to feel a hibernation of sorts, a withdrawal from the affairs of his house and farm. He grew quieter as a result, and more passive when he wasn't active, not like a hibernating bear but like a bear waking from hibernation, or like a day when the sky was cloudy, or like a slave again. Like the slave he'd been on his best days, who knew how to work his master even when he was worked. He'd actually learned to welcome the increasing distance and insensitivity to his life—the distractions of so many thoughts just drifting away. He wasn't there yet, not fully, but soon he'd be up on his toes for what was happening solely and immediately outside of himself so that his mind could decide without deciding, just instant action. *Tick tick.* Able to do things sometimes that surprised even him, glory to God, as if what he was now, praise Jesus, was a slave not to men but rightly to Almighty God. To *God.* Which was why, maybe, the Good Lord didn't let Bass forget, even in his forgetfulness, that without him he wasn't so smart, he wasn't so much. A bullet could own him, too.

3

Tamales

Buggies and wagons of happy folk joined Bass and his horses on the road to Fort Smith. Laughter filled the air where hoof, wheel squeak, and the smells of dust and gloom didn't. Otherwise, the streets cleared of business, with shop owners beginning to shutter for the noon hanging.

Strawberry quickened his gate when the stone fort wall came into view in the bend of the river, with the red-brick two-story federal courthouse peeking watchfully over it. While everyone else rode into the yard to tie up their horses or park their trucks as close as possible to the courthouse to begin their trek to the gallows on the bluff, Bass pulled Strawberry off the road to approach the grub wagon and the empty prisoner wagon he'd hoped to find waiting along the fort wall. Willy Leach, his cook, and Floyd Wilson, his posseman, were on time for a change.

"We need us a bullfight," Bass heard Willy saying before he could see him, blocked by the covered supplies behind him. "We wouldn't be scared to kill bulls here, not in Fort Smith."

"They didn't even kill *one*?" Floyd asked.

"Not *one*," Willy said. "Fact, the bulls had no fight in them either. Get stuck with a couple darts and they was charging for the chute to get out. A whole town a cowards you ask me."

Bass walked Strawberry up on Willy's side, and the talking stopped.

"Boys," Bass said, and the three tipped their hats.

"Hey, already went inside and grabbed the writs for you," Floyd said, reaching inside his coat pocket. "I saw a warrant with Jim Webb's

31

name on it. I was hoping he didn't really jump. I was hoping he'd just show back up, say he was ready for trial. Was just running late."

"Be nice that way, wouldn't it?" Bass said.

"So you think you know where he is, or you wanted the warrant just in case?"

"I think I know."

"I don't mind saying, I don't much want to see that character again." Floyd leaned over the side of his seat to pass the stack of writs to Willy and spit between the wagons.

Willy took the papers and handed them to Bass but without looking at him or speaking. Willy was an old slave set in his ways who never looked anybody in the eyes for long, but since he relaxed around Floyd, always looking up or over at him, even briefly, as he spoke, Bass was always hopeful of a blooming. Of course, Floyd, though white, wasn't in charge, and that probably had a lot to do with how Willy was.

"I appreciate you giving me a second crack at Webb," Floyd said. "I know I messed up good last time. Just froze. That wasn't like me."

Bass nodded. He flipped through the writs to make sure he had enough blank ones before tucking the papers into a saddle rider. He looked back at Willy, who was bowed with his short neck and barrel body, solid as a stump, and staring off at his horses, maybe stewing over the injustice of having been a slave and whipped to mush. His past was the reason Bass kept hiring Willy as his cook and not someone more pleasant.

"So you went to Dodge City after all, did you?" Bass asked him.

Willy lifted his face without actually looking at Bass and frowned. "Yeah, and had fun at first, drank a lot, cut up, you know, but I went for the fight and nobody died, not even the bulls. Not nary one."

"And all that fuss," Bass said. He watched Willy wave gnats from his mouth. "Y'all want a biscuit?" He pulled out Jennie's bundle of biscuits, still a little warm to the touch.

"Sure, I'll take one," Floyd said, so Bass tossed him one.

Willy shook his head. "I'll wait for tamales. We staying, ain't we?"

Bass wiped his mustache from the corners of his mouth, first the left side then the right. "Today ain't Christmas," he said, hoping Willy would look at him, Negro to Negro, and when finally Willy did, Bass said, "Paying our respects, and heading straight out." He packed the biscuits, except for one, and took a bite.

Willy shrugged. "Prince of the Hangmen will pull the trap, you know he will, and hell or high water, Mexicans will be selling two-penny tamales. Something to count on is all."

"Hear a Seminole's dropping with the Coldirons," Floyd said. "You know him?"

Bass turned to him and placed the rest of the biscuit into his mouth. He dismounted. "Nuh-uh," he said.

"Dang it, should be Webb's time today," Floyd said.

"Should," Bass said, still chewing, tying Strawberry to a wagon wheel.

Floyd and Willy hopped to the ground, and Floyd waved a finger at the bay Bass was towing. "Good-looking bay. Think you'll need him?"

Bass shrugged. "Webb in a running mind." He struck out across the yard, like so many others.

Floyd jogged to keep up with Bass's long strides, while Willy trailed behind.

"I like me some tamales though," Willy said.

"Me, too," Floyd said. He looked at Bass. "Don't you?"

"Yeah, but who don't?" Bass said.

They walked in silence along a footpath through the side yard, past enough idle livestock to support a regiment. Bass remembered the noise of war, then heard a grackle somewhere on the roof of the courthouse or in a tree, its metallic song winding up like a steamboat cranking up an anchor. With rain coming, he noticed more slugs were out than usual, clinging to the whitewashed limestone foundation of the courthouse, always trying to find their way into the rank jail in the basement.

He slowed as he rounded the corner and looked down the backside of the building, toward the portico and the jail doors below it. A gathering of turnkeys, deputies, reporters, attorneys, and the rector from Saint John's milled under the portico and on the steps. No one stood straighter in a pack than James Mershon, with shoulders as stiff as a ladder rung. Of the deputies, James was Bass's closest friend.

Bass looked over his shoulder at Floyd and Willy. "Wanna come say a word with me?"

Floyd scratched a sideburn. "Maybe next time, boss. Don't much care for them Coldirons."

Willy pointed ahead to the gallows and the concessionaires, who had set up their carts outside the privacy fence, and kept walking.

"No dillydally afterwards," Bass said, and he turned and walked on toward the portico, watching again for a black veil or for long strands of graying black hair. He hoped to stay clear of Mrs. Coldiron, today and forever.

"Bass! There he is," James Mershon called from the portico. He laughed as he descended the steps to meet him.

Others called to Bass and waved and Bass tipped his hat.

"I was just telling your story," James said, swinging his arm from his hip in an exaggerated drawing motion to shake hands. "Funniest thing how you arrested those Coldiron boys. What you think of!" His red mustache, bushier than Bass's, hung low and covered half of his smile.

"God work in mysterious ways, don't he?" Bass said.

James laughed as if Bass were making a joke. "Congratulations to you, Bass."

Bass nodded but didn't like the tradition of thanksgiving on hanging day. Any other time James would remember that, but like most others on hanging day, he got too giddy to be himself. Bass leaned in, and James's bright blue eyes looked cracked. "You seen their mama?"

"Yeah, she's around, so keep your ten-gallon low. She hates you something awful, Bass Reeves. I mean, *awful*."

"She has a right to, I guess." Bass noticed Lester, the young turnkey with wispy blond hair who always smiled when talking about his wife and young daughter, and motioned for him to come over.

"Friendship wasn't exactly how we left things, you know?" He gave James a pat on the arm before he stepped away to speak to Lester.

"Would like to say a word to the Coldirons right quick before we get started."

"Shore," Lester said. He reached for his key ring and turned toward the jail door to the right of the portico. The two jail cells beneath the courthouse were identically cavernous. They could hold up to 150 prisoners each, and on either end, for shreds of light, was a row of four grated windows, square as soda crackers, two on either side of their doors.

Lester glanced back. "You doing good today, Bass?"

"Can't complain." Bass followed him down the steps to the door. "How's your little girl? She good, I hope."

Lester rattled the key into the lock but looked up from it to grin at him. "She throws an arm or leg across me at night. Cutest thing. Across both us. Gotta know where me and her mama is at all times."

"Stretched out like baby Jesus, ain't that something?" Bass said. "That's the best, ain't it? So free and easy."

Lester blinked slowly and nodded. "You right." He turned the lock, then shoved the door open, and urine stench gusted against them as solid as a bed sheet, like the light they threw in.

Bass removed his hat and stepped into the gated lawyer box, which on hanging day held prisoners scheduled for execution, and his head nearly grazed the ceiling planks. He saw the Seminole first, sitting on a blanket with his hands and legs in irons—his youthful face as blank as a face could be while squinting.

"Hers ce," Bass said, greeting him. He watched the Seminole's eyes shift from his badge to his open coat and six-shooters. The grit hissed between Bass's boots and the flagstone floor as he turned and walked to the other side of the box, where he found the brothers slouched beside each other, also in irons and on blankets but with their heads down, their faces hidden by their dark, tousled hair.

Black, red, and white faces emerged above the Coldirons from the dark cell beyond the bars of the lawyer box. It was loud as a hot night back there, with an insect-like constancy of wheezes, pants, and snorts.

Bass tipped his head and looked down at the brothers. "Wayne, Thomas," he said.

Wayne, with the mustache, raised his face first, glistening with sweat, and Thomas followed. His chin hair still hadn't caught up with the adult growth of his sideburns.

Bass waited, letting them speak first, but the boys remained tight-lipped, in no hurry to bad-mouth. So he started, "I wanna pray with you if you like me to."

Both boys stared at him as blankly as the Seminole had, then Wayne shut his eyes and lowered his face again. Thomas didn't move and then he did, jerking his hands violently to rattle the irons.

Bass didn't budge, until he smirked. Then Thomas smirked.

"Bazz don't startle?"

"Don't have to," Bass said. "God watching out. Why I need to?"

"Is he now? Here?" Thomas asked.

Wayne raised his head with wide-open eyes.

Bass pointed his hat at them. "You both did wrong so you paying for it. That's God watching out—out for me and my family and for Lester here and his, and out for you, too, believe it or not. Here's your last chance to set things right. He's watching and he listening. This is it."

Thomas gazed at Bass, was still. He breathed in slowly and blew his cheeks out. "You just so dead sure."

Bass squatted down to his haunches and shook his head. "Some-one dragging me down the road away from my wife and young'uns to come here to speak to the likes of strays like you. Don't I got a noose round my neck, too? Why I gotta come out and hunt boys like you and not farm and be happy with the kind a peaceful life I got? Not a life I gotta get but a life I got! You hear me—*got*? Who's that dragging me down the road? Who tied that knot? If I wrong, Thomas, who then? *Who*?"

Thomas kept on gazing, right at him, but was still, still. Wayne also gazed, but away.

Bass stood and brought his hands and his hat together in front of him. He shut his eyes. "Lord," he said, "you led me to these three young men so I can try to lead them to you. I pray if they hadn't started to open up to you yet, they will here directly on their last walk out to the gallows." One of the prisoners in the cell beyond began a hard spray into a urine tub. "I pray," Bass continued, louder, "that as they climb those white steps of the platform, it's like they climbing up to you, Lord. And I pray they take their knot like your hug and shrug their earthly shells quick as your grace can come, with no pain, Lord, only feeling your hope, your forgiveness, your love, your everlasting time, like a choke of cold water. There's quite a drove out there, so I pray you three boys will show them something beautiful, something amazing, they ain't never seen. Amen."

"Amen," chimed Lester behind him and the prisoners crowding around the box.

Bass opened his eyes, and Thomas gnashed his teeth, his jaw muscles bulging. When Thomas blinked, Bass looked away, between the bars to those others listening. Their eyes full of sweat.

Wayne's head bounced, his face hidden; then Thomas turned his face back behind his locks.

Bass nodded to the Seminole. "E vketecet owvccvs," he said, meaning, "Take care," which was the closest thing to a prayer he knew in the man's language.

He stooped as he stepped outside and pulled the brim of his Stetson low to his brow. The smells of grass and river and rain and concessions gradually replaced the stench of the jail in his nostrils as he hiked up the bluff toward the sugar-white gallows, whose privacy fence stood sixteen feet high, blocking all but the platform's rectangular flat roof. He looked up at the clouds getting sewn up like a quilt, though a downpour had never stopped a hanging.

A shard of black flashed ahead, and Bass saw a woman turn from the concessionaires and draw a veil back over graying black hair. Mrs. Coldiron's round, solemn face was as round and solemn as he recalled, just as her build was square. She plodded in heels in his direction, though her attention was fixed on the tamale in her hands as she worked to peel back the husk.

He lowered his head and tipped his brim even lower. "Ma'am," he said in passing.

The concessionaires sold something for everyone—tamales, smoked sausage, fudge, both raw and boiled peanuts. But Bass didn't like to eat at a hanging.

He paused before passing through the gallows gate and turned to watch Mrs. Coldiron, seesawing and biting and chewing, almost hobbling, downhill.

Most of the spectators, especially fathers and their boys, congregated elbow to elbow at the gallows platform, where George Maledon already waited, quiet and petite and very neat in his black suit, wearing his pistol belt as always outside his buttoned coat. His deep-set eyes gave him the appearance of being tired, as if he had trouble sleeping, but he claimed he didn't. He was checking and double-checking his nooses. Bass knew him to be dedicated to his work. George would prepare the nooses the day before, making large knots because that ensured a broken neck and a quick death. He didn't like a gruesome strangulation on his gallows, not with women and children looking on. He even tied a large knot in his tie, but you had to ignore his cloud-white, cloud-shaped beard to notice.

Bass didn't like to attend hangings. Whenever he did attend one, he stood in the back, against the fence. At six foot four in boots, he was tall enough to see what he wanted. Willy and Floyd were shorter by five or six inches, being as tall as most people, so they always pressed closer to the platform, where he spotted each of them now, holding then dropping their empty husks.

4

Twelve

Once the bell at Saint John's Episcopal began tolling up on North Sixth, the crowd at the gallows began to count in the hour. More and more joined in so that by twelve there was quite a chorus. As if at a wedding, heads turned in a hush toward the gate to see the procession. The rector entered first with the newly appointed marshal, John Carroll, a former Confederate, so Bass didn't trust him, even if his deceased wife had been a quadroon, and he didn't like that wide white part Marshal Carroll kept in his short, oiled hair, like a remembrance, or that jutting brow that hid his eyes. The Seminole and the Coldirons entered the yard in single file. Mrs. Coldiron entered next, then Lester and two other turnkeys followed her and closed the gates.

When the rector and the marshal reached the platform, the marshal touched the rector's back and spoke briefly to him before stepping aside to join Commissioner Stephen Wheeler at the front of the crowd. The rector pointed toward the steps without looking back at the prisoners, then took them first. The Seminole followed, but the Coldirons paused without words to take a hug and a kiss from their mother. Mrs. Coldiron visibly shook as she pulled her veil over her face and slipped into the crowd out of view.

The court had already spoken, so the hanging was essentially a wordless ceremony. The prisoners walked up to a noose, and George tugged it down over each prisoner's head as if it were a Guernsey jumper. All three prisoners could have been brothers from the mutual shock in their eyes as he tightened each noose with a yank.

Once George had strung the men, George raised a hand to the rector, standing at the end of the row, beside the Seminole.

The rector recited the same prayer at every hanging, drawing upon verses from Micah, so Bass no longer heard many of the particulars. Bass heard or rather felt the wash of his own pleading interpretation: *Lord. Lord? Lord! Lordy Lord.*

Nothing reminded him more of being a slave than being shut in this white castle to witness the termination of wasted lives. To clear his mind, he repeated his prayerful meditation: *Lord. Lord? Lord! Lordy Lord.*

Once the rector had said Amen and dabbed his lips with one of the oblong tabs of his white clerical collar, George bellowed the few official words necessary for all to hear—the Seminole's name and crimes—and then he asked for his last words.

The Seminole shook his head, so George called Wayne Coldiron's name, listed his crimes, and asked for his last words.

Wayne openly wept as he gazed into the crowd where his mother had gone, lost from Bass. "I love you, Mama."

"Stop your blubbering!" she cawed at him. "You're stronger than that, you hear? You're better than all these people."

Wayne squeezed his eyes shut and choked with tears while heads turned in the crowd, doubting what they'd heard.

"Stop it, I tell you!" Mrs. Coldiron's disembodied voice insisted.

"Thomas Coldiron," George yelled, having had enough of the nonsense. He liked a hanging to click along and was hot-tempered whenever it didn't. He began to list Thomas's crimes, but Thomas interrupted him.

"Enough already, I did it, I did it all," Thomas said, turning red and turning to George. "Sooner we get this hanging done the sooner that woman will shut the hell up. My whole life she just rattles on. Fuck it, let's go!"

The crowd erupted in cheers that drowned out Mrs. Coldiron's pleas for something.

George didn't have to be begged. He stepped back and reached for the lever. When the trap doors flung open with a heavy cough, the ropes already squealing, Bass turned for the gate.

◆ ◆ ◆

Bass waited with Strawberry and Fringe for Floyd and Willy to reappear, jogging through breaks in the crowd, as rain began to fall.

Floyd climbed up onto his wagon seat and exhaled a laugh. "Sorry, boss, but that was a good'un."

"Made up for Dodge City, sure enough," Willy said, climbing up onto his.

Bass tilted his head back to soak up the scent and tick tick of rain. "Get ready for bad weather, boys," he called and clicked his tongue for Strawberry to jump ahead into a trot, to get out in the lane before more horses and carriages and wagons wouldn't let them.

It was as if God disapproved that men should have to spend their lives hanging men like the Coldirons or chasing men like Jim Webb instead of staying home and was pressed to show it with air and rain that smelled and tasted this sweet from other places.

So to the mud under hooves, Bass decided to sing. "God's wrath is with me, on my high horse beneath me." He liked the cadence of his verse, a new one, so he sang it again, only louder. "God's wrath is with me, on my high horse beneath me." He wished Jennie were seated at her piano up on the boardwalk on Garrison Avenue, play-ing something to go under the words as they passed.

Needing another verse but not knowing where to go yet, he started with repetition, remembering in the slave quarters how that was Uncle Moseley's way when stuck. "On my high horse, my high horse, I ride by so many saloons and whores, but worse are the happy death-watchers, watch them shut up their doors."

He started to miss the first verse, so he went back to it. "God's wrath is with me, on my high horse beneath me." Then he missed the second one. "On my high horse, my high horse," and then, as the rain began to whip, he wanted to add something new. "I ride straight for you, Jim Webb, and I will get you, of course."

"Sing it!" Floyd bellowed, above the rattling of chains and fall of rain, the slosh of wheels missing ruts.

So Bass sang it, digging in:

> Do you hear my steed's hooves, do you see the clouds
>   rain?
> Jim Webb, are you listening, I've got a writ bears your
>   name.
> Jim Webb, Jim Webb, why you running again?
> Don't you know running free without a right is one devil
>   of a sin?
> So heed this warning, old friend, if you decide once more
>   to shoot.
> We will make the same money just by bringing back your
>   boots.

This time Floyd joined him at the top, but that was all there was left, as the outskirts of Fort Smith fell back and they passed the cast-iron U.S.–Indian Territory border markers, shaped like smokestacks, like stove pipes, what Bass called "Hell's pipes"—just the top, as the rain stole the sound right from their mouths.

5

Scrambled Eggs and Brains
and Ripe Cantaloupe

Bass led his outfit across the Choctaw Nation in a southwestern diagonal, following the Butterfield Overland Trail, camping for the night in the valley of the Narrows in the Sans Bois Mountains. A day's ride from the Dead Line, this remained over the years a safe place to rest. The stream provided good drinking water and was deep enough for a bath, if he was of the mind to bathe, which he rarely was this early out, and he wasn't again tonight. He chose instead to change out of what he called his ownself clothes to put on even dirtier ones. Webb had never seen him in his tramp disguise. Webb may have heard about it from other prisoners in the wagon, from the Coldiron brothers who wouldn't have kept quiet, but tramps of all sorts were as common in the territory as antelope.

What Webb would more likely recognize, and from a distance, was the prisoner wagon, so while Floyd unsaddled the horses and fed and watered them at the stream, Bass cut branches from a weeping willow. To keep the chains and leg irons from bouncing along the floorboards, he wrapped the branches around them and tied them in knots.

After a couple of weeks of being dragged through the territory and watching the wagon gradually fill up around him, Webb had unexpectedly spoken. They were in the Seminole Nation, near Little River. Willy was setting up his equipment at the campfire, preparing to cook, and Bass and Floyd were discussing the next day's plans of picking up two thieves in the custody of the Seminole Lighthorse

Police in Wewoka and hunting down Little John, a whiskey peddler in the Creek Nation who'd recently murdered a deputy. Webb
hadn't spoken since his arrest.

"Some rumbling tumbling tumbleweed you got here," Webb
decided to say, his words nearly growls, from where he sat in the
shadows, chained by a leg and a wrist to one of the wagon wheels.

Bass regarded him without a word, and as though Bass had asked
him to explain himself, Webb tipped his head back and knocked it
twice against a spoke of the wheel.

"The thunder gives me a fucking headache," Webb said.

Remembering that moment tonight in the Narrows, Bass hauled
himself into the bed of the prisoner wagon and jumped up and
down. It squeaked under his weight like any wagon would, but it
didn't rattle from the irons. "Maybe now," he said, "Webb won't hear
ole Tumbleweed coming up on him, even if he's laying in the road."

"In case he got dog ears to go with that dog face?" Floyd said.

"Maybe. I don't know. I cotton to dogs," Bass said. He hopped
down and waited for Willy to bring him a pan of beans. The sun
had set over the treetops of the Sans Bois Mountains, and the night's
first bats were looping above like big flakes of ash caught in a gust.

◆ ◆ ◆

To arrest Webb the first time, he'd woken before sunup, before anyone else, and pulled out his straight razor and a triangular shard of
saloon mirror he'd picked up years earlier after a brawl and shaved
the itch off in the firelight. He'd no longer be a tramp on the run,
who he'd needed to be to arrest Thomas and Wayne Coldiron. He'd
now be a traveling cowboy with his traveling cowboy companion,
so he could afford a little comfort. He'd still have his unwieldy mustache and the freckles peppering his light-brown cheeks, so his face
would be clean but not too clean. He'd have the look rather of a dis-
tinguished derelict—somebody with nothing to steal. And someone
with nothing to steal was no one to bother with, and no one to fear.
This same look he wore at home and took to church.

Wearing denims and dusty boots, he buttoned his leather cuffs, buckled his gun belt with both pistol handles pointing forward, and put on his black coat and black ten-gallon Stetson. If Jennie were there, sitting on a rock or log, she would go on about how good-looking he was, and would hug and kiss him. Her hands wouldn't leave him. Of all his disguises, the cowboy was easily her favorite, while his was easily the tramp, even if the shoes weren't worth anything for walking a country mile in. He liked remembering when he was broke and had nothing. He liked knowing he wasn't anymore, and he liked knowing people underestimated him. He liked coming from behind, being the salt of the earth. He felt most like Jesus then. As a cowboy, he felt most like God. He would have to remind himself he wasn't.

In the left pocket of his coat he carried a Sheffield bowie knife in a buckskin sheath. When he carried it, he always carried it in his left pocket so he'd always know where it was, just as he always kept his rifle scabbard slung on the right side of his saddle, his catch ropes on the left side, and his revolvers always holstered handles forward for a cross-draw—not only so briars and underbrush couldn't snatch a trigger and shoot his horse dead beneath him, but so he could always expect his pistols to be where he reached. Unless he had reason undercover to alter a pattern, he preserved it, always—always his weapons in the same locations.

Willy fried potatoes and boiled coffee, and still before sunup, Bass and Floyd were mounting their horses.

The Washington-McLish Ranch was one of the oldest and largest and most profitable ranches in the territory, owing to Dick McLish's Chickasaw ancestry and political connections and the ranch's convenient location a few miles northeast of the Chisolm Trail's main entry from Red River Station, Texas. Moving herds east of Texas had been a boon ever since the end of the Civil War. A steer that sold locally in Texas for five dollars could collect as much as forty in the northeastern markets, and the Chisolm Trail took most of them up to the rails in Abilene, Kansas. To move the herds, the Washington-McLish Ranch hired up to fifty cowboys at any given time, and Webb's reputation as a foreman was that he ruled them ruthlessly with his fists. To protect his cattle and their grazing land, he was willing to do anything. Even kill his neighbor, a Black circuit preacher, for allowing a small grass fire to get out of hand and cross property lines.

The duty Bass had been charged with was one of the more extraordinary developments of his forty-five years. Here he was, Judge Parker's most trusted deputy, a Black deputy, pursuing the arrest of a prominent white man for killing a Black man. Times had changed, all right—right along with the rising value of beef.

According to the description the victim's wife had telegraphed the court, Webb stood five feet, nine inches tall, had dark, sunbaked skin with deep vertical wrinkles in his cheeks that looked like scars, and typically rode a bay gelding with another bay gelding in tow.

Bass recognized the spare horse as an old strategy among Indians avoiding capture. Once you exhausted one horse, you could change onto the fresh one and easily elude your captors on their own exhausted horses. So Bass took precautions against Webb's precaution, planning to catch up with Webb off his saddle at the ranch house during breakfast.

Floyd rode beside him on a gray mare. He chewed tobacco and slouched his shoulders. They rarely spoke this early, not until the morning behind them had caught up to the west in front of them, but by then they were almost at the ranch.

"We'll ask for breakfast," Bass said.

"Makes sense," Floyd said.

They arrived at eight o'clock, the overlapping w-m brand carved into the cross-posts of the white gate. Cowboys were already out in the open pastures herding cattle into separate pens for branding and castrating, while flocks of red-winged blackbirds feeding on grass seed picked up like cyclones, one after the other, and resettled out of the way. A dirt path rutted by wagon wheels led to a log ranch house, with the bunkhouse and dining hall connected by a long dog run, where three men sat on shadowed benches. Across from the ranch house, beside a barn, a blacksmith pounded iron in his shop.

"Hope we ain't too late," Floyd said. "I'm starting to get hungry."

Bass surveyed the pastures once more as if merely wiping his face on his sleeve. He prayed those cowboys minding their work kept minding their work. There were a lot of them. He admitted, "A sausage patty sound good."

"Don't it?" Floyd said.

They dismounted, tied their horses to the rail outside the barn, and walked toward the ranch house. The blacksmith's hammer behind them was steady, and their steps fell into its rhythm.

Two of the three men in the dog run rose to their feet, arms casually hanging by their sides, pistols in their right hands.

Midway in the road Bass held up a hand in peace, still unable to see any face well enough yet, but race-wise and size-wise, they could all be Jim Webb. The blacksmith paused in his work.

"Morning," Bass said.

"Howdy," Floyd said.

The man standing on the right nodded his head, but no one in the dog run spoke.

Bass stopped at the base of the porch steps and removed his hat. Now he could see the man on the right had black furrows in his sun-leathered face, like he'd been swiped twice by a panther. The man on the left was just the man on the left.

"We a bit far from where we gotta go today," Bass said, "so we was wondering if it wouldn't be too much trouble to oblige you for a little something to eat for me and my buddy, Floyd, here?"

Webb on the right tipped his head. "Where's a bit far?" His voice was deeper and raspier than Bass had expected from a man his size, as if he'd once survived a hanging.

"Got ranch work in Montague," Bass said. "My oldest there. Thought we might meet up."

Webb's small gray eyes looked away toward the barn, toward the blacksmith, who was now hammering again. Then he motioned with his pistol for Bass and Floyd to step up, and Webb backed away, telling the man seated on the bench to cook them up something.

The other man, whose pistol hung by his side, followed Bass and Floyd under the roof of the dog run. The door to the dining hall was propped open by a limestone brick, like the limestone bricks mortared in the rear kitchen chimney. The cook went through first, followed by Bass and Floyd and by the two with their guns drawn.

"We appreciate this," Bass said.

"Sure do," Floyd said.

Bass dipped his hand into his pocket and slapped a silver dollar on the nearest table before pulling out a chair and sitting. "We aim to pay, though. We ain't broke. We ain't begging."

Webb shook his head.

"Really, we want to," Bass said. "Or *I* want to." He smiled. "My friend here don't care."

Floyd shrugged. "Free or not, it'll taste the same—am I right?"

Webb shook his head. "Free always tastes better." At the end of the table, he pulled out a chair, and his friend did the same.

His friend had a half-smoked cigar tucked behind his ear. He was the only one in the room not wearing a hat, the only one with a beard, the only one who hadn't spoken yet.

"Y'all got a big ranch," Bass said. "Is one of you Washington or McLish?"

"Shit," Webb said.

"You Mc*Wish*, huh?" Floyd said. He laughed and elbowed Bass, and Bass smirked at Webb and Webb's friend, and Webb's friend smirked back.

Webb's friend propped his feet in the seat of the chair beside him and nodded. "That's a good one," he said.

Webb continued to eye Bass with suspicion.

"You know, since this is gonna take a little while," Bass said, "I should go on feed the horses. You don't mind, do you?"

Webb didn't blink. He shook his head. "Corn meal's free, too," he said.

"Suit yourself," Bass said. He stood up, plucked his silver dollar off the table, and heard Webb stand up and strike his bootheels across the floor behind him.

Webb followed from a distance as Bass unhitched the reins from the rail and led the horses into the barn. Webb waited at the barn door while Bass stalled them and loosened their saddle girths and filled their feed troughs. Bass even removed his Winchester from his saddle scabbard and leaned it against the corn crib, hoping to convince Webb to trust him, that he meant him no harm.

Bass strode the length of the barn with a smile, while Webb stood his ground in the light of the doorway with the squared stance of a man ready to raise his weapon and fire. At any movement of Webb's right hand and barrel motion, Bass could dive off in the hay and draw later. That would be his best option. With each step he took that Webb didn't move aside from his stance, Bass was ready to dive off in the hay—beneath a wagon, beneath a horse, behind a stall door, behind a saddle stand. He was ready to dive off when the cook called out from the ranch house that breakfast was ready. Bass was ready.

"Music to my big ears," he said to Webb.

At point-blank range, too close now to Webb for Bass to dive off, Webb's best chance to kill him, Webb stepped back and let him pass.

Bass crossed the road and took the porch steps, but Webb was slow to follow, his footsteps mute in the dust. When Bass entered the dining hall, he found Floyd eating from a plate of scrambled eggs and brains, and Webb's friend still sitting where he'd been sitting, his pistol still in his hand but held listlessly in his lap. As Bass sat down, he saw in the mirror across the room that Webb had taken a seat on one of the benches in the dog run.

Bass sighed and dropped into his chair. "Looks good, don't it?"

"Uh-huh," Floyd said without raising his head.

Bass said a silent prayer as he pulled his plate closer to him. He glanced again at Webb in the mirror as he chewed his first bite. What he'd done with the horses by unpreparing them for chase must have gone a long way to convince Webb he really meant no harm.

"Cully," Webb barked.

Webb's friend, Cully, slid his boots off the chair they were propped in, scraped his chair back, and scuffed out.

Floyd kept eating, and so did Bass, but Bass ate with his head up, watching Cully in the mirror pass through the open door and join Webb on the bench. Webb whispered and Cully leaned in.

Bass looked toward the kitchen for the cook, but the cook was gone. He reached for his cup of coffee, and Webb was gesturing toward Bass and Floyd with wider eyes and a lift of his hand.

"When I signal," Bass whispered, and he made a sucking sound through his teeth, "you take Cully. I'll jump Webb."

Floyd laid his fork on his empty plate, then sucked his teeth in confirmation.

Webb and Cully didn't appear to hear them, but they were settling down, no longer gesturing or whispering, both quietly facing the backs of Bass and Floyd.

Bass picked up his fork again. The brains were bland. He preferred them seasoned with peppers and onions.

Webb and Cully hadn't moved in some time.

Floyd leaned on his elbows, sipped his coffee.

Bass finally put his fork down and reached for his cup once more and took a sip.

"Pretty good eats," Floyd said.

Bass swished the coffee around his mouth as a rinse and swallowed. "Yeah, pretty good for free." He wiped his mouth and mustache on his sleeves, first the left side on his left sleeve, then the right on his right, then rubbed his hands on his pants legs to make sure they were dry and quick and wouldn't slip.

Floyd slid his chair back.

Bass glanced at the mirror as he stood and turned, and it was as if Webb and Cully were statues of cowboys sitting on a bench.

These were the moments Bass lived for—as if the moments themselves cracked open their yolks, and in that slow time there was nothing but energy. The energy of good will and evil intentions, bucking like mustangs on a level field. When God allowed him to hear and see and feel what God did.

He stepped out first into the dog run and patted his stomach, a small excuse to have a hand so close to gripping his six-shooter. "Much obliged, gentlemen," he said, "much obliged."

Webb nodded stiffly, his small eyes bulging—more blue now than gray. Bass could see he was ready to do anything, shoot a man in the back, any man, to get rid of his fear and feel right again.

Bass crossed the dog run and sat down on the second bench against the bunkhouse wall, on the end closer to Webb. Floyd sat on the opposite end. Bass looked over at Webb. "If y'all ever looking for good help," he said.

Webb nodded through a delayed pause. When he spoke, he spoke with a forced evenness: "I make room for good help."

Bass nodded. "Good to know."

"Yep," Floyd said.

Cully struck a match on the sole of his boot and stoked up his cigar.

By the length of time the blacksmith had hammered without a break, Bass wondered if he was forging something long and useful for himself like tongs.

"You know, on second thought," Webb said. He stood from his bench, his revolver still in his right hand by his side. He walked over to Bass, who was still patting his stomach, and stopped in front of him. "If you don't mind," Webb said, "I think I will have that silver dollar."

Bass looked at Webb with steady eyes. "Course," he said but without moving his hand from his stomach to retrieve it. "I got more than one, though. How many you want?"

Cully stood up and walked around Webb, his revolver also in his right hand by his side. He stopped in front of Floyd, his cigar tucked in the corner of his mouth.

Bass smiled. "I always keep a few dollars on me because my baby girls love them, just love them. I give them one every time I come back home. My boy likes *things*, like a saddle or a gun or something, but my girls, now they have a thing for silver. Really do. Course, they younger."

"Just one," Webb said. He gazed at Bass, and Bass nodded but didn't move yet to retrieve it. "If you're gonna work for me someday, I can't let you believe I'm a pushover. The one's enough."

"Now, come on," Bass laughed. Webb's eyes were locked on him, while Cully's darted back and forth between Bass and Floyd, leaving Bass with no opportunity to suck his teeth. "Who would take you for a pushover?" he said. "You seem fair, but you seem tough. No, sir, no pushover. Not like me with my young'uns. That's why I'm still traveling all the time like a damn young man. I should be settled down on my own farm raising cattle and growing cantaloupes and corn and such, you know? You know what I'm talking about, right?"

"You giving me that dollar?" Webb said.

Bass stilled his hand on his stomach. The blacksmith had stopped hammering. A sulfurous hiss of yellow pig iron cooling in tub water carried across the air, and Bass believed he could smell it.

"I know you ain't asking for more than the one," Bass said, "but I want to give you more than it. I want to give you some advice."

Webb's muscles constricted throughout his whole body so that he looked an inch shorter.

Bass glanced at Cully, his brown eyes as hard and small as rusted nail heads, his cigar forgotten in the corner of his mouth.

These two clearly thought his advice was a warning of violence.

Bass returned his attention to Webb and paused for a breath. "Ever fed your horses on ripe cantaloupe?" He smiled, instantly seeing the letdown in Webb's eyes. "Gives them a burst of energy like nothing else. Better than cornmeal even, no joke, and happy! Man, I'm telling you, happy."

A cough from the road almost startled Bass into turning—then Webb turned, his jerked profile an opportunity—so Bass lunged. With no time for signals, he grabbed the barrel of Webb's pistol and wrenched it out of his hand, flinging it clattering onto the porch and thrusting his left hand around Webb's throat, wrapped completely around it like a bandanna, choking him, as he whipped out his Colt with his right hand and jammed the muzzle against Webb's clenched left eye.

Webb burbled sounds of giving up.

Bass held firm and looked away to see how Floyd was handling Cully, but Floyd hadn't moved at all from the bench. His weapon was still holstered, while Cully's was raised, aimed high at Bass's head.

Before Bass could react, Cully pulled his trigger and the gun cracked red, discharging a bullet that whizzed past Bass's ear. After the kick and in the smoke, Cully aimed again, quickly, lower this time, toward Bass's torso, and fired.

Smoke streamed from the barrel, but Bass didn't feel a strike and he didn't wait to feel one. He drew down on Cully with his Colt and blew him backward with a .45 slug to the gut. Cully's pistol dropped to the porch with a thud, his cigar dropped with a bounce of ash, his gut bloomed like flowers.

Bass turned toward the road to find the blacksmith in his leather apron, with coal soot on his face, scrambling to get away in a cloud of dust. Bass looked back at Webb, purpling in the face. "Get handcuffs on this one," he ordered, and finally Floyd roused to a hustle, jerking off one of his boots to produce hidden irons.

Cully bellowed, grabbing his gut, dipping his hands in his blood.

Floyd locked the cuffs on Webb, but Webb wasn't fighting, except to gasp for air. When Bass let go of his throat, Webb crumpled to his knees, coughing and wheezing. Bass searched him for more weapons. Then he searched Cully, and made a pile out of reach.

Floyd shook his head. "Don't know what happened."

Bass stood over Cully and watched him slobber and writhe. Piss had spread down both thighs. "I saw a wagon in the barn. Go hitch it up, and be sure to grab my rifle. Left it up against the corn crib. We best get this one to a doc quick."

A porch board creaked beyond them in the distance, and this time Floyd reached for his pistol and joined Bass in aiming. The scared face of the cook peered around the corner of the dining hall.

"We the law," Bass said.

The cook pulled back out of sight, and his boots pounded in retreat, but even as the sound grew faint, the beating grew back again without him, into a rumble, a quake far louder than sound.

Bass sidestepped Cully and Webb, and Floyd followed him and looked with him up the road at dozens of horses galloping from the pens and pastures and filing toward them on the road. Their trailing dust merged into a mountainous cloud that fattened before it thinned and, for the briefest moment, darkened the sun.

Some of the cowboys were white and Indian, but most were Negro, and though all had guns, none raised them in defense of Webb or his friend, choosing instead to clot the road flank to flank until the wagon in the barn had been hitched and loaded and needed clear passage out. Few spoke, as if humbled by what they witnessed. Then Webb shouted for them to get back to work—hoarsely, spitting blood. And with no more words, they did.

6

The Dead Line

He rode ahead of the wagons but was still in sight, in the moonlight, as if he were twenty years younger, newly free, and once again a low-rent scout hired on short notice along the Butterfield Overland Trail. After two long days of riding through Indian Territory, the Dead Line was finally upon them, just beyond the bend, that last tree line.

Bass's eyes roved the wooded darkness for any spot of torchlight, any slippery movement, anyone with wrong ideas—absorbing what he saw as if reading. On each flank he read the darkness and darker darkness between here and there of scattered trees and scrubs, intertwining slopes, then turning in his saddle, the unreeled plain behind them, leading far back to the Sans Bois Mountains. The total circumference of their observable world seemed as clear as one could pray for.

For good measure, he assumed more of his tramp disguise, letting the good posture of his shoulders and erect back melt his recognizable stature into a loose arc that gave languidly now with every other stride of his sorrel.

A cicada swarm droned in the tree stand of the bend, vibrating the air, and above the silhouette of treetops, the moon sat plump, flattened only slightly on one side like a cantaloupe.

Bass hadn't spoken for hours, though behind him Floyd and Willy had been shouting back and forth from their wagon seats all day.

"You see, because his daddy's a Mick," Floyd said, "that makes him a Mick. Doesn't matter if he was born there or not, Canada or not, Vermont or not. So that tells me, since we don't know for sure about the other, President Arthur's a Mick and only a Mick."

"Hold up, now," Willy said. "We know he ain't only a Mick cause he here and be a citizen."

"Nobody can be a citizen of more than one country," Floyd said. "Especially a president. Willy, he's got to belong to one law and one people. You got to put your hand on the Bible and swear yourself to one."

"I ain't arguing with you on that," Willy said. "You damn can't be both because that Mick/America shit cancel each other out. That's what I'm saying. And if that Mick/America shit cancel each other out, then you know what that make our president?"

"Canada's president?" Floyd cackled with laughter, and Willy tried to speak over him.

"Nah, nah, Floyd, wait up. Hear me out. What I'm saying is he ain't nobody with a right to be or do or say or put his hand on nowhere nothing. Because that dual-citizen shit cancel each other out. And since they ain't no treaties to speak of to protect a man who come from nowhere, that no-country bastard can be shot dead by anybodies. Right here on this road right now by you or me, with no badge or not."

Their debate faded to silence, and Bass was pleased. Most people stopped talking this close to the Dead Line.

With his fist holding the reins, Bass wiped his mustache from the corners of his mouth, while still rocking on his sorrel, still reading the darkness. He watched the bend gradually dissolve and reveal the unlit station house no more than fifty yards away, the rails of the Missouri-Kansas-Texas Railroad glistening in the moonlight like running tear streaks. In the distance were skeletal signs of a store and three houses.

He pulled up on the reins, and once the wagons squeaked closer, he walked Strawberry into the clearing toward the station house. At this late hour, the station house reminded Bass of a cicada shell, hunched mute and frozen on its porch posts. Something forever vacated, like so little of the West anymore.

If someone were perched in hiding atop the station house, he probably would have first noticed Strawberry, hearing the soft stamps of cracked unshod hooves, seeing the river-shaped blaze, a bluish night-white thickening as it wound to the nostrils. As the horse emerged fully into the clearing, that someone, if there, might have noticed that the sorrel was actually sizable, up to nineteen hands tall, appearing perhaps too large for the slouched rider. Perhaps, too, the rider appeared drunk or much more tired than he was— either way, a scout too undisciplined to be taken seriously. Unless that someone perched in hiding was Webb.

Bass had learned from the Seminoles to embrace what he hunted, as if he and his prey were not ahead and behind but bound on the same journey by an invisible yoke. Seeing from the eyes of the hunted, while listening to the beat and song of its heart, would cut down on tricks and tragic mistakes and increase bounty. And it had. In nine years as a deputy, Bass hadn't once been ambushed.

And he'd learned to embrace the Twenty-Third Psalm. He used to recite it over and over, hundreds of times in a row, mindlessly for miles. Now, cautious but unafraid, he just walked through the shadows.

On the day Judge Isaac Parker had ridden out to Bass's Van Buren showplace on a stallion as white as his beard and the snow on the ground in January of 1875, he told Bass as they sat before the fire in the parlor that only the most fearless and foolhardy of peace officers would pursue wanted men across the Dead Line. "To preside over the largest federal jurisdiction in U.S. history, seventy-four thousand square miles spanning more than a dozen Indian nations, I will need to hire a host, if not a horde, of deputies and pray they're all more fearless than foolhardy. I'm starting with you, Bass," he said, "because I hear you are the bravest and least foolhardy of anyone living."

Nearly fifty of his fellow deputies had been shot dead since 1875 and most of them west of these tracks. Posters nailed on the posts of the station house glowed like tombstones.

Bass cocked an eye at the first poster, obviously snagged from its original nails. It was a wanted poster his own Western District had printed and distributed but now, typical in the territory, it had been flipped to its blank side and reposted with a boastful warning from the wanted man to the lawmen on his trail. Bass could read people and things, even some things that were hardly things—fire, blood, clouds, tracks—just not words. But he knew what names looked like, even the many incarnations of his own, since Floyd worked with him, studying writs by firelight.

He scanned the crude handwriting on the poster, and when nothing familiar emerged from the shapes, he looked to the next poster, and the next, until his name finally surfaced like a fish from the murk. There were more words on this one than most outlaws bothered to write, with the last word beginning with the letter that resembled a gar's bottom front teeth, followed by two moons. If *Moore*, as in Chub Moore, it was not a good sign.

He eyed the poster below, and although he didn't find his name, he found a name he recognized, spelled with a gar's top front teeth, a hook, and two skyward-pointing pistols: *Webb*, he was certain. He reached out and with two flicks of his arm tugged both posters free.

He wheeled around and bypassed Willy, who couldn't read either, and held the posters out to Floyd, who could read almost anything without stumbling.

Floyd held the first poster out in front of him at a slant in the moonlight and squinted: "From Chub Moore."

Bass nodded. "What he say?" He'd been trying to catch the Chick-asaw outlaw for seven years, ever since Chub Moore incited a mob to lynch a Negro man for raping a white woman from Texas who was visiting family in Cherokee Town. He'd since killed others, too, including a Choctaw cohort who'd given Bass information on his whereabouts, but Indian-on-Indian violence didn't fall under the jurisdiction of the Western District of Arkansas. That fell under the jurisdiction of the Lighthorse police in whichever tribal nation the crimes had been committed, and the Lighthorse were poorly equipped to apprehend criminals running from nation to nation. Perhaps Chub Moore had grown restless for action. This was his first communication in a long time.

Using his tongue, Floyd worked his wad of chewing tobacco back against his cheek, then leaned over the side of his wagon seat and spat. "Let's see. He says, 'Deputy Bazz beware! Cross the line once more and I will hang you from my skinning tree and after I plow the earth with your bones and soak cabbage seeds in your blood I will deliver a cabbage feast to my children and my children's children so that you will carry in the spirit world the stench of their shit forever.'"

Bass smirked into his mustache. "Glad to hear he's turned to farming."

"Damn crazy," Floyd said.

"He'll have to wait. I hope he can stand it."

Floyd shuffled the posters. "This one's from Jim Webb. Ain't that timely, like he knows we're coming."

"For two thousand dollars, why wouldn't we?"

"Ain't addressed to you or any of us by name. Oh, hold up, it is, too." Floyd looked up at Bass and offered a jagged grin. "Get this, 'Sleeping with skunks don't make you a friend of mine Mr. Nighttime. Next time you die.'"

"I don't think he likes me," Bass said.

"Ha," Floyd said. "He's a damn crazy one, too. Course, we knew that." He handed the posters back, and Bass unbuckled the saddle rider where he kept his book of writs, coin purse of silver dollars, and photograph of Jennie, taken the year he was deputized. He folded the posters together three times and tucked them inside as case evidence.

Bass clicked and clipped ahead of Floyd and the prisoner wagon, with two spare saddle ponies in tow, then ahead of Willy and the grub wagon, and continued in silence along the Butterfield Overland Trail. He led his outfit past the station house stockyard, where off-loaded cattle from Texas were temporarily held for watering and trading, and out of the clearing, into more trees—hickory and oak and pine, among calling owls. They would camp for the night by the cold spring creek he called Corn Creek, which split cornfields just minutes away. Bass remembered the site fondly from many previous runs, at times smelling hominy from kettles simmering downwind from the Choctaw clan that lived nearby, and so Strawberry must have remembered, not tempted in the least by the muddy troughs in the stockyard.

◆ ◆ ◆

"The thunder gives me a fucking headache," Webb had said, growling as he spoke, prompting the Coldiron boys to snigger.

Bass recalled that he stood up from his bedroll in front of the low, red fire and looked down over the fire at Webb, who leered at him from his seat on the ground against the wagon wheel, the deep ruts in his cheeks absorbing the shadows. The bruised imprint of Bass's hand on his throat had faded, but at night it was still dark enough to make his head appear to float.

Bass consulted the Coldirons, shackled to a shackling log. They made childish faces at him, and Thomas Coldiron fought to free his hands. It was an ongoing habit he'd developed over the last couple of weeks, and no longer trying on the sly, every few hours, as if the act would eventually spook the colored deputy into believing the young killer could summon devilish powers, suddenly break free, and vanish like a ghost.

"Simmer," Floyd called.

Bass tipped his head down at the dirt and walked around the fire, around Willy clenching his teeth, rinsing the prisoners' plates and forks and cups with water he'd boiled in the coffee pot but itching to stop and draw his revolver, a silver-plated Smith and Wesson he was quick to brandish and slow to reholster. Bass didn't like the look of it, the ornate engraving and ivory grips. It reminded him too much of his old master's ivory-gripped Colt Dragoon, though he never saw Master Reeves polish it each night before sleep the way Willy did his. As far as Bass knew, Willy had fired the piece only a handful of times, and always at a varmint—a snake, a rat, a turkey buzzard.

Thomas and Wayne followed Bass with squinted eyes as he approached and then passed them.

Off behind the wagons the horses dreamily munched their oats.

Bass stopped in front of Webb. He brushed his coat open and set his hands on his hips. "I want you three knowing why I'm taking you in," he said, "and it ain't just what's on those writs. That's why the law wants you, but why do I? Other than the money, I mean— and the money's good, don't get me wrong, and y'all make it good indeed. But how do *I* make it good?"

Webb continued to gaze where he'd been gazing, as if Bass still stood on the other side of the fire, while Wayne looked down at his own lap and rolled his bottom lip over the straggled ends of his mustache, while Thomas locked onto Bass with a sneer.

"Think about what you see in the daytime when you look up at the sky," Bass said. "You don't see stars, do you? You see blue color and clouds, too, and the sun and sometimes the moon, but mostly it's that solid blue straight across, like the surface of a lake. Weird, ain't it?" He tipped his head back and pushed his brim back to look at what appeared to be a lake itself, the sky banked all around by treetops. "There the stars are at night, but during the day they hid." He lowered his head and corrected his brim. Webb hadn't budged. Wayne stared only at his boots or at dirt or at nothing. Thomas continued to sneer and simmer, as if that alone could untrack Bass's mind.

Bass returned Thomas's stare with a smile. "That's like how God be. Sometimes you see him, and sometimes you don't. But that don't mean he ain't always there, ain't always watching you." He nodded and eyed Wayne again, still stubbornly gazing down. "I imagine you feel you ain't seen much of him in your life and that's why you got caught up in what you have. Well, that's the day. You ain't seen him, but he there. Fact, he here in me right now talking to you. Why I want y'all to think of me as Mr. Nighttime, because night or not, cloudy, don't matter, I be bringing you the news of his presence and his glory and his law."

Thomas snorted long, dragging his sinuses clear.

"Boy," Floyd said, "you spit that on him, I will get up from here and bleed you out if he don't."

Bass kicked the sole of one of Wayne's boots. "You don't say much." Wayne tensed his shoulders but refused to look up. "You must be scared. You must be hearing me."

"Go to damn hell, Mr. Nighttime," Webb said.

The Coldirons whipped their heads toward Webb and laughed. Thomas spat in the fire.

Bass backed away and saw Webb still staring vaguely ahead, over the fire, as if preferring to remember Bass at some point in the past to actually looking at him. "Boys," Bass nodded.

He stretched out on his bedroll, next to Floyd on his, and shut his eyes under the tilt of his hat. He always slept best in camp after emptying his heart. Sleeping as if he were under the open night with his own family.

Whenever he dreamed of home, he dreamed of his first home in Van Buren, on the old Reeves plantation, five and a half miles northwest of where he lived now. Jennie and the children would sometimes be there with him, with his mother and auntie in the slave quarters, along with Jennie's piano and her braided rugs and draperies and pictures and their longcase clock. And though the walls would be painted buttercup yellow, the splintery, unpainted door with the rag-filled knothole would stand there untouched in his memory, permanent as Heaven. Sometimes he fell asleep praying he'd dream of home.

He wasn't there yet when he heard a hiss and a rattle of handcuffs. Without stirring his head or legs or hands, he let only his eyelids move, his eyes adjust.

Thomas was sitting up and leaning forward off the log, baring his teeth and hissing at Bass. And then he stomped his bootheel in the dirt and hissed again.

"What the hell's wrong with you?" Floyd asked.

Thomas fought his irons, and now his brother was rousing with a start. Thomas eyed Bass's hands or his guns maybe and stomped his boots.

"You best settle down before I get up," Floyd said.

Thomas elbowed his brother and began the most obnoxious ballyhoo, and now Wayne chimed in with his own yelps and hog calls, eyeing Bass, too, but not really Bass directly. His bed directly or his legs.

Bass looked down his body and slowly eased up his head to find a curl of black-and-white-striped fur pressed against the crook of his left knee.

Floyd and Willy hollered for the prisoners to get quiet, but the Coldirons got louder, and Bass could feel the skunk waken, its body stiffening in fear against his leg.

"It's okay," Bass cooed. He slid a hand down his leg and gently touched the skunk's back. "Okay? It's okay," he said, petting it.

"Jesus, it's a skunk!" Floyd said.

"A skunk?" Willy shrieked. "Where? Where?"

Willy and Floyd darted away in the shadows with a flash of silver, and Webb, somewhere on the other side of the fire, growled laughter.

"Step aside, Bass," Willy said, "and I'll kill it before it sprays. I'll kill it."

"No, no, no," Bass coaxed. "It's okay, ain't it, fella?" He stroked the animal while the Coldirons continued their racket in a brazen attempt to stoke a fire from it.

"Hush up, fools!" Floyd said.

"Yeah," Bass said, as the skunk rose up on its paws and turned its snout to Bass, its plume tail up but not all the way. "We good," he told it. "We good, ain't we?"

The skunk swanked away without a scent, gone to the trees.

Bass looked at Thomas, silenced by his own disappointment. "You was conceived in an ill season for sure, boy."

"Damn crazy," Floyd said.

Somewhere on the other side of the fire, Webb continued to laugh. If Bass had sat up all the way, he would have seen him. He would have seen that floating skull. Only he closed his eyes.

7

There Were Cattle

Bass didn't always follow the same route, stopping in the Narrows and again later at Corn Creek to camp. In fact he'd done that only twice before as a deputy. Apprehending the Coldirons and then Webb in April of last year and then hunting down Webb again now demanded this coincidence, which felt like order and brought a calm upon him he didn't usually feel this side of the Dead Line before he'd apprehended anyone. He didn't need to get cocky and careless, and he told himself he wouldn't. He remained calm, knowing his routine in the morning would change.

At sunrise, instead of helping Floyd tack the horses and hitch the wagons while Willy fried breakfast, Bass rode out to the village a half-mile away, where the Choctaw clan of maize farmers had made dugout homes of mud and corn husks, with pitch roofs made of pine planks coated with pine tar. The men heard Strawberry's gallop and walked out to greet Bass at the road.

Bass knew enough Choctaw to say, "Halito, chim achukma?" He waited for their polite response, which dependably followed. So he said his mother loved hominy, rhythmically and rhyming, despite his chopping tongue: "Sa-ishki holitopa tansh lakchi." Then he asked what he could buy for a dollar: "Kanohmi achaffa dollar o?"

The men whispered, and the oldest of them stepped forward. He stood barefoot and erect like the others but wore more tattered clothes, more tattered even than Bass's tramp disguise. His gray hair parted on the side was cropped short like a white man's. He raised a fist at Bass and stuck out his thumb. "One sack, one dollar," he said in Choctaw. He added two fingers. "Three sacks," then closed his thumb, "two dollars."

Bass opened his saddle rider and found his coin purse. The sacks could be five-pounders, a bad deal for him, or ten-pounders, a fair deal. The Choctaws had always been fair, so he didn't ask. Since his mother apparently couldn't have too many servings of grits, he plucked two silver dollars from his purse and reached out to lay the coins in the elder's outstretched palm.

The elder looked at both sides of each coin, then turned to a young man in the group, the only one who wore his hair in a long braid. "Tuchena," the elder said—the number three a smoky murmur.

The young man with the braid left the group to speak to the women standing in the doorway of one of the larger homes, surrounded by naked children. The women and children stared at Bass before disappearing into the home behind the young man.

After that no one spoke. Everyone outside watched the empty doorway. When the young man reappeared, three twenty-pound burlap sacks lay across his arms and covered his face. The women and children followed and gathered again at the doorway.

The young man walked diagonally to see his way, then stopped beside the elder and eased the sacks to the ground with the cinch side up. The elder leaned down and uncinched one to show Bass what he was buying—whole kernel hominy, which Bass could mill into grits for his mother himself once he'd returned home. But *three* twenty-pounders to tote across the territory?

Bass shook his head no. "Tuklo," he said, holding up two fingers.

The men mumbled words too low for Bass to hear, and the elder offered to return one of the silver dollars.

"No," Bass said. "Tuklo, tuklo," pointing his two fingers at the coins in the elder's hand and then at the sacks. Two twenty-pound sacks for two dollars would still be a bargain.

The men gazed at him without expression, as if unsure if their guest understood he was cheating himself of a better bargain.

Bass nodded and patted his lap, showing where the young man could toss the hominy.

Because this clan sold hominy to the Chickasaws, Bass asked the men if they had seen or heard of a red white man, a rancher, by the name Jim Webb, and Bass curled his hands into claws and ran his fingertips down his cheeks.

The elder looked at the other men, and they looked at him. Then the elder looked back at Bass and tugged his ear.

"Within the last few months?" Bass asked in Choctaw.

The elder nodded.

"Alone?"

The elder's head twitched. It was hardly a reply. "Yummut wak uhleha tuk," he said, saying, "There were cattle."

"Washington-McLish amiti yo?" Bass asked.

"A," the elder said.

Bass nodded, wondering if the elder might know or admit knowing the whereabouts of another. "Chub Moore-ato katimma yo?"

"Ak ikháno," the elder said; he didn't know.

Bass looked away to the other men as if their faces told otherwise. They continued to betray nothing, but Bass bumped his eyebrows up all the same and half-grimaced before returning his attention to the elder. "You saw Chub Moore?" he asked—"Chub Moore ish pisa tuk o?"

The elder turned to the others, and the men shook their heads. The elder tipped his face back up to Bass. He didn't blink. He didn't breathe. Then he took a step closer. The postmaster in Cherokee Town. He told Bass to speak to the postmaster in Cherokee Town.

Bass tipped his hat to the elder and to the others. "Yakoke," he said, thanking them.

◆ ◆ ◆

He regarded the young maize fields to the left and right of the road—so many thousands of green sprouts on brown rows that flowed away as if forever. He squinted, and it was how an ocean might look when the mind remembered. Each one of those plants would grow to become so burdened with life it would want nothing more than to lie down and die, like the hominy in these sacks across his lap, yet there was so much hope for them now.

He passed the barbed-wire fence he'd passed earlier, and it was still as peculiar to his eyes as telegraphic lines were if he looked up and saw stripes on the sky, as if it were a shirt. Cattle too skinny to be cattle were chewing out one hardscrabble existence, like everything else.

Fourteen years had passed already since the House Committee on Indian Affairs had initiated a civilizing policy for about nine thousand Arapaho, Cheyenne, Apache, Kiowa, and Comanche Indians who had been relocated to the Indian Territory just west of the Chickasaw Nation. To prevent the Indians from returning to the plains out of starvation, Congress approved an annual subsistence of 730 pounds of beef on the hoof for every man, woman, and child. As a result, beef-issue days on the reservation had become both carnivalesque and sacrosanct. The first time Bass had attended one was in November of 1870.

His friend Old Caesar, or Caesar Bruner, a Black Seminole rancher and band chief, had won the bid to supply the cattle to the Cheyennes and Arapahos that month. He'd been sixteen in 1829, when he walked the Trail of Tears from Florida to the territory. He eventually settled on Salt Creek in the Seminole Nation and founded Bruner Town, where he found Bass, in 1862, standing and shivering in rag clothes splattered with patroller blood at the edge of a meadow with pistols in his hands.

Bass was waiting for the dark Negro Indian man with white hair and earrings to turn his buckskin Spanish mustang away from his inspection of grazing Longhorn calves to notice him there at the edge, between meadow and creek. Bass needed everything—food, clothes, refuge. All he'd eaten after escaping his master's plantation in Texas three days earlier was raw turtle meat. For payment he had the two pistols he'd taken from his master and overseer—a nickel and ivory Colt Dragoon .44 and a Smith and Wesson .22, which he held at the ready as if they couldn't possibly be empty.

Four other Black Seminoles, on dun, grullo, and roan mustangs, joined in a semicircle about Old Caesar. They were younger, in their twenties like Bass, and spoke in a tribal language Bass hadn't heard before.

When Old Caesar at last noticed Bass, it was their secret. Old Caesar calmly studied him as he had the calves, before walking his mustang from the group and approaching the creek. He was a lean and slight man with unlevel eyes; his left one was positioned a little higher than the right and was slanted like a Chinaman's.

Bass stood straighter and tightened his grips. He checked on the others, but, like the elder, none sat on saddles with rifle scabbards or even had a pistol out of its holster.

Old Caesar stopped his horse two horse lengths away. "Istonko," he said. The half-circle of riders looked over but without panic.

Bass remembered "hello" from the Cherokees in General Pike's First and Second Mounted Rifles whom he helped train at Fort Washita during the war, so Bass said, "Osiyo," to let the man know he was friendly to Indians. Maybe the man would also notice the beaded necklace they had given him.

"Seminole?" Old Caesar asked in a voice that was deeper than Bass's despite his size.

Bass shook his head, afraid he'd lost his way and hadn't reached the Seminole Nation after all, not if this elder could mistake him to be a Seminole. "Slave," Bass corrected, which appeared to delight the man.

"Seminole," Old Caesar repeated. "Runaway, yes?" he asked, nodding insistently.

Bass smiled now at the young maize on waves, at the old memory of him and Old Caesar reaching an understanding for the first time. He patted the hominy across his lap. "Jesus a-coming and I's a-going," he began to sing in no more than a murmur. "Praying for that Heaven place."

Seminole had been the first of many words that Old Caesar and later Old Caesar's wife, Nancy Lincoln, would teach him.

Yes, Bass had once been a Seminole. Now, he wasn't. Now, Jim Webb was one.

◆ ◆ ◆

That November, in 1870, Bass had helped herd Old Caesar's cattle to the Darlington Agency, a few miles northwest of El Reno on the Chisolm Trail, where the agency clerk distributed them to the head of each Cheyenne or Arapaho family. Crowding the beef-issue pen were squaws wearing blankets about them, while men wore beaded leggings and moccasins and shirts and vests, sometimes neckerchiefs. Their hair hung down in two long braids, whether man or woman or girl, and the braids were tied at the ends by strips of pelt, or the hair was gathered and bound in a shiny large knot on the forehead and pierced with a hawk or turkey feather, while the boys wore their bangs cut short in a jagged line. And everyone wore red ocher painted along the parts in their hair to honor the path of the sun, to indicate that one found happiness at the end of a road, that the arrival of food was fated.

Once the wide-eyed, thin-lipped agent from Pennsylvania, with short roan-like hair, called an Indian's name in halting, tinny syllables, Bass or one of the other hands would release the Indian's allotted steers into the adjacent prairie, and instantly that Indian's family began to yip and howl—not in pursuit yet, to relive the plains, but because the cattle were too tired and hungry from the trek to play buffalo, so they were scared and slow to leave the chute.

Bass or one of the other hands would prod the steer out with a branding iron, and the Indian men would leap after them on horseback, armed with bows and arrows. That's when the squaws would throw off their blankets, revealing hairpipe chokers and dresses decorated with rows of elk teeth, and take off on foot, waving hatchets. The hunters would gallop alongside a steer and aim for the heart or lungs, and once the moaning, chuffing steer dropped, the squaws would fall upon it, hacking off the horns and hooves first, then skinning and butchering it into silence. The children would join in then, begging for the vitals.

The families would work all over the foul-smelling prairie until sunset, until every bone and scrap was stacked efficiently high on travois and their horses and dogs cleared them out.

8

Webb Again

The humidity intensified as Bass and his outfit trekked into the Chickasaw Nation, the land flattening and softening, with so much water crisscrossing. They rode almost entirely in a mute knot, with Bass and Floyd on the flanks with rifles at the ready. If anyone they passed had thoughts of holding them up, they quickly thought better of it.

Unlike the other Civilized Tribes of the territory, the Chickasaws did not welcome freedmen as citizens of their nation—not even those who'd lived in their villages since birth. The Chickasaws were racist and proud. They were taller and fairer and fierce, and though they had great disdain for everyone else, they never declared war without great deliberation and smart allies. They had again and again defeated the mighty French, after all, which explained why the U.S. government didn't position the Chickasaw Nation along the border of Arkansas, preferring instead to keep the most peaceful close at hand. As a body went west, the tribal nations grew incrementally more aggressive and unpredictable, as did the non-Indians who dared to live among them.

For this reason, Bass cautiously avoided all villages, leading Floyd and Willy on a circuitous path, traversed from his own memory and design. Not that Bass feared an organized attack, not on a deputy marshal conducting business beneficial to the Chickasaw, but there were always rogues on the main trails who demanded tolls, and he didn't need to slow and risk the attention to busy himself with penny fish. There were more of them everywhere than a body could count.

♦ ♦ ♦

By noon they'd reached the outskirts of Tishomingo, the Chickasaw Nation's capital, and were passing the patch of dirt where Bass and Floyd had buried Webb's gut-shot partner, Cully Smith, who'd finally bled out right here only moments before reaching a doctor. The grave a year later looked to be nothing more than an ant mound.

By sunset they had already pulled their horses and wagons under the cover of a hickory grove beside a lake outside of Ardmore, about ten miles southeast of Bywaters's Store, where Bass had reason to believe Webb was hiding. Arlin Bywaters had posted the seventeen-thousand-dollar bond to have Webb released, and more horses than necessary had been observed tied outside to the porch rails or to a shade tree. A man with dark, maybe Mexican, skin had been sighted there almost daily, and he always rode with two horses.

Floyd and Willy wasted no time stripping down to wash off in the lake. Bass was slow to follow, considering what change of clothes to take. Bass knew he couldn't fool Webb again. He could slip up on him maybe but wouldn't fool him. Webb had seen the cowboy and maybe the tramp, if he or his men had spotted Bass over the last couple of days. He could now be expecting him to appear in that form, but he'd never seen Bass as Bass. So Bass set out his ownself clothes and scouted the area first on foot before joining his men in the water.

Diving under, he thought of those Choctaw children standing in the doorway that morning, dry as they could be, then those two sacks of hominy, which would need plenty of water to soak in. How delighted his mother would be. He sang without thinking about what he sang—not even hearing Jennie's voice, just hearing his own but, like a memory, hardly hearing even that:

It's a place I'd die to taste,
Praying for that Heaven place . . .

Hominy was an easy thing Pearlalee would never let him forget, saying "yakoke" in her own way, over and over.

◆ ◆ ◆

Many of the deputies of the Western District had long believed that Bywaters used his store as a cover for a whiskey trade. Peddlers with connections to Bywaters had been arrested and convicted over the years, but Bywaters had never been directly implicated. If he was involved, he always smartly used handlers. And why would any of his handlers ever turn on him when it was Bywaters who paid their bonds and lawyer fees? He could easily recoup the money from a thriving whiskey trade, not a two-penny general store. A fifth-gallon bottle sold in a U.S. state for two dollars had a resale value of twenty dollars in the Indian Territory, and still whiskey produced even greater profits.

A whiskey trail less than a mile from Bywaters's Store ran north into the Arbuckle Mountains, and like a seam on up to the northern boundary of the Chickasaw Nation, conveniently close to the Washington-McLish Ranch. With Webb's connection to Bywaters now revealed, and his continued connection to the Washington-McLish Ranch through cattle drives, Bass suspected Washington and McLish were involved in the whiskey trade as well. They were probably smuggling the whiskey in from Texas with the cattle and giving it over to Bywaters to manage distribution. It made little sense any other way.

"Unless," Floyd said, "Webb was working independent of the ranch. A side business Washington and McLish didn't know nothing about. Just him and them cowboys, you think?"

Bass weighed the idea as he settled his head against his saddle and pulled the brim of his Stetson down low, level with his eyes. He remembered how indifferent those cowboys were. Willy sat on his bedroll across from him, polishing his silver-plated revolver. Around the lake the frogs sang. "But would Webb be worth seventeen thousand dollars to Bywaters," asked Bass, "without a sure connection anymore to the ranch if the ranch is who's driving the whiskey in?"

Floyd let his silence hang over the question, thick as tree cover, thick as no moon and no stars. Just frogs and Willy's rubbing.

◆ ◆ ◆

"They need you, too."

Bass opened his eyes, unsure of how long he'd been asleep, but the fire, like a clock, quickly told him.

He turned to Floyd and then to Willy on the other side of him to see both were dozing. The fire in front of him was down to licking its chops. It would soon be a closed-mouth simmer, and after that, it would soon be day. Bass took a calming breath and shut his eyes anyway. He saw Jennie and her disapproval and thought of those words he'd tried not to hear, as if Jennie had uttered them right here in the nation and not at home just before he left.

Of course, their children needed their father, too. Jennie didn't need to say it, not with evidence like Bennie to point to. All a body had to do was show him to the jury and wait for them to churn in their seats into butter.

Caesar occurred to him again. Caesar had told him stories about Negro Fort, where he was born and his tribe of freedmen had lived until he was three, near the mouth of the Apalachicola River, only sixty miles from the Georgia border. The British had built the fort in Spanish Florida at the beginning of a war Bass had never heard of, then abandoned it to the freedmen, maroons, colonial marines, and runaway slaves who manned it. Hundreds of Blacks lived there. It was their fort, their town, their way of life—a bright pearl in another ugly oyster or, better yet, Caesar had said, a basket of gallstones in golden brown cubes and pyramids one was lucky to find at the end of a cow's slaughter. Slaves trickled in from as far away as Virginia. The only white people a body saw were remembered ghosts, who were exactly the sort to fret about every threat to slavery.

Caesar's earliest memory was of the day he saw white faces for the first time, and they were hellish, unattached to bodies, floating in and out of flames and columns of pitch-black smoke, as he'd told Bass that first night he'd given Bass refuge, allowing him to sleep on the floor with his children. The day the Americans invaded Negro Fort with sabers and muskets, with no hands or arms or legs, with only faces, those sand-white faces, had also been the last day of the fort's very existence.

The American gunboats had advanced upriver to begin firing upon the fort, but the fort had an arsenal of cannons, too. Each side volleyed with increasing success—hitting only water but striking closer and closer to their targets, until an American cannonball hit the fort's powder magazine. Seminoles in Pensacola, a hundred miles away, would later tell of hearing the explosion. Caesar said charred body and long-rifle parts were strewn in a bountiful display of all shapes and sizes. Caesar sat silently on a cold hearth, smoking a pipe when he wasn't talking. Then he shook his head without a tear, saying sometimes he made himself see his people as the Americans had seen them—as gourds populating a field without a purpose until you fashioned one. He said Bass should do the same and never forget it.

On the floor with Caesar's children, Bass imagined a Negro Fort nation without state or territory boundaries, where everyone wanted to live in a field, together in peace, so white people had bodies and limbs and Negroes were their equal. Squash and melons and gourds alike. Bass wanted America to be that way, but everywhere in America and not just in a fort or part. He wanted it with all his might. Negroes beyond his ability to count them all now relied on him to help make that happen. *They need him, too, Jennie*, his heart told that simmering fire.

◆ ◆ ◆

After breakfast, Bass reminded Willy of his instructions not to leave the grove and of what to say if anyone were to come by asking questions. "You under orders from Deputy Mershon to stay put," he said, "and say he won't be back for a day or two."

"Right, investigating horse thieves from Ardmore," Willy said. "Got it."

"That's all you know?" Bass said, testing him.

"All I know. Hell, I'm just the cook," he said with a smile.

"Well, you know what the man looks like, what kind of man James Mershon is, though, right?" Bass said. "I mean, you work for him, don't you?"

"He a white man, sorta like you, if that's what you getting at," Willy said.

Floyd shook his head and tugged his hat down low.

Bass smiled to play nice. "What else?"

Willy shrugged. "Got a mustache. Don't you all?"

"How big a one?" Bass asked.

"Big," Willy said.

Bass nodded. "What else? How tall is he?"

"A few inches taller than me, I'd say, and that only because I ain't got no neck, but even with a neck he ain't as handsome as ole Willy N—— Leach." He scrubbed his bearded chin with his long fingernails. It was still his notion that a beard and long nails made the master and therefore the man.

"What you mean 'not as handsome'?" Bass said. "The way you say it sound like Mershon be uglier than ugly. Like he can't be no more ugly. That he needs you to help explain just how ugly he be. That what you saying, Willy?"

Floyd was laughing but Willy wasn't. "I mean what you know I mean," Willy said.

"So he ain't that tall then, huh?" Bass said.

"Nah, not tall," Willy said.

Floyd threw his hands in the air. "Willy!"

Bass hung his head, his hat blotting out all of Willy, down to his boots.

"Willy," Floyd said, pushing his hat back out of his eyes, "you're supposed to say the man's tall, for goodness sake."

"Well, I wouldn't say a man tall because he a few inches taller than me. I ain't shit for height. Hell, Bass, you the one tall."

Bass raised his head with a nod. "Exactly, Willy."

"Exactly," Floyd said. He punched Willy in the arm. "That's why he wants you to say Mershon's tall, so you don't seem like Bass's man, get it? Like you don't know what tall is."

"Oh, okay, I get it, I get it." Willy placed a hand on his belly as if he were bracing it to keep from falling. "Why didn't you say so?"

◆ ◆ ◆

Through the morning Bass and Floyd and their three horses passed through grazing herds of cattle over grasslands bursting with grasshoppers. On the edges, antelope scampered away for what few trees there were. Until there were more and more trees dividing the grasslands, at the foot of the Arbuckle Mountains.

Bass had stepped foot in Bywaters's Store on two occasions, once as a cowboy buying tobacco and the other time as a tramp begging a meal, and had spoken to Arlin Bywaters both times. He was a heavyset man with a grizzly beard who sat on a stool behind a register and never moved from it, except to turn his head. He'd take your money and give back change but would bark orders at some lackey to do the fetching.

For the last mile, they avoided the road, taking trails through the woods. They stopped where the woods broke into a clearing, giving them a view of Bywaters's Store, about fifty yards away. It was a log-and-mud structure with one plate-glass window overlooking the porch, to the right of the door, which stood open. To the left of the door hung a sign, the store's name brush-stroked in royal blue. A bareback pinto, spotted black and white like a cow, waited at the rail without being tied, its tail whipping at flies, and across the clearing, tied to a yellowwood tree, were two bay geldings, nibbling at leaves.

A Chickasaw man, evident by his height, as tall as Bass, walked through the door onto the porch carrying a ten-pound sack of flour tucked under his arm and gripping a brown whiskey bottle. He took the single step to the ground and climbed onto the pinto and rode off, holding onto its mane with one hand.

"Walk up to that window," whispered Bass, "and if you see Webb, wave me up and hold there. If he ain't, run on back."

Floyd nodded, chewing his tobacco fast.

"If either one draws to fire, then go ahead," Bass said. "Kill 'em."

Floyd dismounted with his double-barrel. He twirled the reins around a branch, looked up at Bass and nodded, then jogged in a crouch to the side of the store, jouncing his coat tails.

Bass raised his Winchester and trained it on the window, then the open doorway, then back to the window, but nothing in them moved that he could see. The bays tied to the shade tree blew with boredom, and so did Strawberry and Fringe and whatever Floyd called his mare.

From the woods, Floyd seemed soundless as he hauled himself onto the edge of the porch. He crept along the front wall to the window and swayed in place like a tree as he peeked in.

Bass took a breath, realizing Floyd had forgotten to take off his hat. That his brim might show.

Floyd stepped back from the window and raised a hand for Bass to come up.

Bass removed his hat to return the wave, and Floyd clutched his hat and tossed it behind him off the porch. This was why Floyd was his posseman.

Bass fitted his hat slanted down and snug on his head, as Floyd took his shotgun in both hands and crept forward again to the window to peer in.

Bass slid his Winchester back into its scabbard and trotted Strawberry and Fringe from the woods. "The Lord is my shepherd," he recited to himself. "Strawberry my horse. I shall not want." Sometimes he improvised.

He wouldn't ride past the open door. He'd ride up on the side with the plate-glass window, presenting no threat at all, his face mostly darkened under his hat like that doorway. And if Webb were to step up to the window to try and pick him off, Floyd could pick him off first.

He watched the doorway grow, forty yards away now, when a reflection in the window rolled by like a cloud. Bass trailed his eyes to see it—the cloud moving fast, maybe too fast to be a cloud. Then the blue-brown blur burst through the glass, a man in a running leap spilling shoulder first.

Floyd sprang back from the crash and falling shards, the hard thump of boots, while Bass spurred Strawberry and reached for his Winchester.

A rifle emerged from the rain of glass, already keenly aimed at Bass from below those deep facial lines.

"Surrender," Bass shouted, trying to sight a shot.

Expecting the crack of fire, Strawberry ducked his head low in great digging strides.

Webb fired, and Bass felt the bullet strike beneath him. He braced for Strawberry's collapse, but Strawberry didn't fall. He kept racing, and Webb jumped off the porch in a run for the horses at the yellowwood tree.

"Under arrest, Webb," Bass hollered, turning Strawberry past the doorway to cut Webb off.

Floyd charged after Webb, the boards barking at his boots. He looked about to shotgun-blast Webb in the back when Floyd pivoted at the doorway and fired up.

Bass heard Bywaters before he saw him filling the doorway with wails, a dropped pistol, his face blown off, a blood swipe above a beard, before he staggered back inside.

And then Webb, again—hesitating, realizing, it seemed, what Bass had already reckoned, that he wouldn't reach his horses, after all. So Webb slid to a stop in the dirt, bravely posting up, and in quick succession levered another bullet in the chamber and fired before Bass could adjust his aim.

The bullet whizzed close, cutting the reins, and Bass's driving hand flung back into his face. From the unexpected freedom, Strawberry squealed and bucked, mad with fear.

Bass jumped to the ground, and Webb cocked his rifle ready and fired a third time, from twenty yards, and the bullet grazed Bass's coat, cutting a button into splinters, as Bass spun to find his footing. The sound of the next click-clack told him to drop flat, and as he did the bullet tore through the brim of his hat.

"*You* surrender, Mr. Nighttime!"

Bass rolled over and saw Webb running for the woods. He didn't see Floyd on the porch or know where he went, and inside the store a .44 pistol report was quickly followed by three more and then a shotgun blast. Bass sat up and steadied his rifle. He had Webb sighted crossing the doorway when Floyd rushed out onto the porch sprayed with blood.

"Stop or die stopping," Bass yelled, but Webb wanted none of it, running for the woods and daring them to shoot in the crossfire.

Floyd chucked his shotgun with a clatter and drew both revolvers.

Bass whistled for Strawberry, still bucking and slinging his head to rid himself of his slack bridle and dragging Fringe behind him. Bass had expected to outride Webb, not outrun him, but there startled Strawberry and Fringe went, toward the woods as if after Webb themselves.

Webb looked over his shoulder at the horses hoofing after him.

"Let's end this without any more dying," Bass said. It didn't usually occur to Bass to shoot a man in the back, but this one was tough enough to almost excuse it. He whistled again, but Strawberry wanted none of it.

Like a stick snapping, Webb cocked his Winchester and a casing flew, then he swung his rifle behind him one-handed in mid-stride at the horses coming up and blocking Bass's view. Bass had trained Strawberry not to startle from gunfire, but this was too much today. This last crack sent him charging over Webb, running him facedown and trampling him, until the shot to Fringe's twisting neck caused Fringe to cry for breath and crumple.

Bass stared horrified as the line that tied Fringe to Strawberry went taut, that moment just before Strawberry twisted backward himself, their heads colliding, whinnying and groaning. A pile of horse.

Bass and Floyd took off in a run, from the clearing and from the porch, as Webb crawled for the woods without his rifle. Webb made it to his knees, to the trees, and fired from a pistol they couldn't see.

Bass fell to the ground behind his horses and whispered their names. He stroked Fringe's nose and ears. Strawberry's.

"Why you have to kill my horse?" yelled Bass. He looked over at Floyd, spread across the ground, too, about twenty yards away.

"He ain't dead yet," Webb said. He spoke with pain, through clenched teeth.

Bass signaled for Floyd to go up and around from the backside to flush Webb out, and Floyd began inching away on his stomach.

"I got a writ with your name on it, Jim Webb," Bass said.

"I guessed that much," Webb said.

"I got you last time. I'll get you this time."

"Not easy."

"I don't reckon why not. Don't you want to save yourself? Do right in the end?"

"Save the sermon for nighttime," Webb said.

"I can sermon in the daytime, too. But people listen better at night. You listened."

"Don't bull-mud me, Bass Reeves. I killed a n—— preacher, and I will kill you."

Bass glanced over Floyd's way, but Floyd was gone.

Webb rustled in the underbrush.

"How many more shots at me you need?" Bass asked. He stroked Fringe, panting out his last moments. "I'm waiting," he said, staring ahead of him at the saddle on Strawberry and noticing a bullet lodged in the horn.

The rustling lingered and then the woods whinnied, and Bass realized his mistake. "What can I do to make you want to come in?" he said. "Talk to me, Webb." He rolled over to reach into his left coat pocket for his knife.

A grunted word from Webb like "Hah!" and Bass knew to begin rolling away before Floyd's gray mare broke through the branches with Webb in the saddle. Webb fired his pistol twice and Bass kept rolling until the fire stopped, then hopped up to see Webb in a gallop for the road.

He had to decide in an instant to choose Strawberry *now*, but without a bridle and without a saddle, too, since that had been how he'd trained Strawberry to ride bridleless, when bareback, or to run across the clearing for Webb's two undersized bays and risk too much delay. Bass bent down and cut the tether between his horses, then the bridle, freeing Strawberry of the bit and calling in an easy tone for Strawberry to rise.

Floyd stomped through the woods, was nearly out, when Bass shoved the uncinched saddle off Strawberry's back. Bass mounted and Strawberry danced with excitement to ride him bareback.

"Shoot my bay for me," Bass called, and with a clutch of mane and a click of his tongue, he leaned forward and then leaned right to guide Strawberry for the western road, still finely billowed with Webb's dust, in the direction of the whiskey trail.

9

High Horse

Floyd's mare was smaller and faster, but Strawberry was stronger uphill and over distance. If Bass didn't lose Webb, he could catch up to him in time. Signs in dust, especially swirls of a circle-back for possible ambush, kept Bass focused, scanning ahead and above and in the breaks of trees left and right. Stopping anyone he passed to ask of Webb's whereabouts would only slow him. Keeping up was all that mattered. Watching to see the dust thicken, at times opening his mouth to taste a difference.

Three miles north of Caddo River, where the trail grew straighter and sloped into a two-mile plain of scattered gray boulders at the foot of the Arbuckle Mountains, Bass could finally gauge his success— spotting Webb halfway to the mountains. A black dot sitting on a churning gray one, spewing up a river of dust Webb wouldn't believe possible, flowing narrow to wide and becoming, in the end, passable breath. Just another river joining rivers, like Strawberry's blaze ever widening to the nose. Even Bass, just another fish in the constant river of fish. "God's wrath is with me," he sang without lips and tongue, just eyes and clenched teeth, "on my high horse beneath me. On my high horse, my high horse," he sang without singing, "I will fear no evil, for thou art with me."

The sun would soon edge the peaks and turn the rock veins violet. Though there was time, there wasn't much of it. He had to close a little more of the gap now in the plain before Webb reached the mountains and could find a perch to shoot from. If Bass could do that, Webb would hope instead to vanish on the other side of the mountains into the night. He wouldn't expect Bass to catch up to him on the other side, but Bass could. In the mountains, he could close what distance remained, but only if he took his portion now.

Strawberry's straight run became faster and smoother than what Bass could ever recall elsewhere. Becoming a perfect bobbing float. Bass understood it and was glad of his choice, even if he were to lose Webb. Freed of all straps and tethers, of the burden of saddle weight and stirrups, of the scene of mayhem, Strawberry finally tasted the truth of being alive and hungered for the whole land before him. He couldn't run fast enough, as if the sun were his apple, his cantaloupe.

When Webb approached the first mountain climb, Bass estimated the distance between them at a thousand yards, better than he'd hoped, but he'd have to reduce that by half to be in range to hit him, even though he didn't want to hit him. He could have already hit him countless times if he'd simply wanted Webb dead. He wanted Webb alive. He wanted him thinking. He wanted him changed. He wanted blackness to save Webb as it had saved Bass.

Remembering the Battle of Pea Ridge, how Master Reeves had regained control of a battle by ordering his cavalry in disarray to collect and advance against greater numbers, Bass waited until Webb had sunk behind the first mountain before firing his Winchester. Something solely for Webb to hear and fear Bass was closer than he'd believed and shouldn't slow and advance in ambush.

When Strawberry reached the base of the mountain, Bass leaned back to whoa him, then leaped to the ground and charged up on foot to give Strawberry a rest, an incline of a hundred yards or so. When they neared the crest, he mounted Strawberry again and rode him over, ready with his Winchester leveled. But seeing the dust cloud trailing up the next mountain, he sent Strawberry racing down.

Halfway to the valley, Bass saw Webb sink behind the next mountain, so when they'd crossed the valley, Bass hopped to the ground again and charged up on foot. Strawberry nickered affectionately beside him. To Strawberry, it was nothing but play.

At the top, Bass again mounted Strawberry and cautiously rode him over, looking first for dust but listening first for horse, and spotting a column of dust again rising like chimney smoke far enough away to lurch Strawberry onward. Webb was beginning to climb the third and last of the mountains on this trail. The distance between them burned away like a wick.

Strawberry raced down the second mountain faster than he had the first, while Floyd's mare under Webb clawed her hooves at the hard trail like an old dog confused by its own death. Webb was killing her. Cursing her to climb faster and kicking with both spurs—his hollow voice carrying throughout the valley.

Thank the Good Lord, Webb must have thought, when Floyd's horse finally mounted that mountain. *Hallelujah, Jesus*, Floyd's mare must have thought as she carried Webb down one last time with no more ups. With that long plain waiting for her, where the sun was likewise driven.

Strawberry simply laughed, mocking Bass as he ran this hard stretch on his two human legs. At the top, Bass could've hit Webb if he'd wanted. But Bass didn't want to be changed by Webb's whiteness. He wanted Webb changed by his blackness. So he let Strawberry take him to him.

Floyd's mare was giving out, thinking, Bass imagined, about that grave the sun was headed to and about lying down there in it, too. Thinking that it wasn't much longer either way. Not with Strawberry grazing at her shadow. Not with Bass in clear range now to take that devil off.

Webb turned in the saddle, showing Bass a skull cheek. He turned back, briefly, and then swung an arm around, showing a flash of pistol steel without much looking, and fired.

A miss but close enough. Bass wanted none of it. He aimed his Winchester at Webb's shooting arm, up at the shoulder, to end this senseless chase, when Webb fired again but without showing his pistol this time, and Floyd's mare folded beneath him with smoke rising from her head and then a fountain as Webb was pitched forward through that mare's blood spurt, toward the setting sun, along with a tumbling loose pistol, before a final slide of his body in the dirt.

Through the sight of his rifle, Bass watched Webb shake and rouse and crawl, then scramble to his knees with his found pistol and raise it one last time at the man floating on the bravest sorrel that ever rode up on death. Bass saw an X in the middle of that man. It was there and chose nothing else but to be proven. Bass had to fire this time, Lord, right now, so he fired, click-clacked, and fired. He lowered his Winchester to his lap to watch Webb fall backward on his legs.

Bass leaned back to slow Strawberry the last hundred yards.

Webb gurgled blood and waved a limp hand for Bass to come closer.

Bass walked Strawberry up, and slid off with his rifle on Webb because this man didn't quit.

Webb sputtered with a mouth filling with blood. He spat and said, "Give me your hand, Bass Reeves."

"Gotta let go of that six-shooter in the other one," Bass said.

Webb rotated the revolver in his hand with the creaky motion of an old mill wheel, until he held the barrel instead of the grip.

Bass leaned down with a knee on the wrist of that hand and took into his hand the hand Webb was offering. "What is it, Webb?"

Webb clenched his bloody teeth and swallowed. "My revolver and scabbard. You must. Take them." Webb's hand was a frail dying thing. All his strength now balled up in his mouth.

"All right," Bass said.

"I killed eleven men with it. I expected you to make twelve."

"You asking forgiveness, Jim Webb? You need to."

Webb coughed blood into a bubble on his lips. "You're a brave n——." His hand tensed in Bass's hand before it went limp again. His eyes rolled and shut, and he breathed crookedly without speaking or trying to for another minute. Red-velvet cow killer ants crawled across his face, curious about those wrinkles.

Bass stood and stomped, wanting none of those cow killers.

10

Somewhere at Sea

The orange sunset continued to redden and purple and the air thicken as Bass transferred Floyd's saddle from the dead mare onto Strawberry. Once he'd tacked him, he bent over Webb, and taking hold of his arms, he dragged the body until Webb's legs had unfolded out from under him and Bass could find Webb's boots. Bass tugged one free, with a cloud of dust, and then the other. From Floyd's saddle he found rope and cut a length. He ran it through the boot loops and tied the ends around the saddle, then unbuckled Webb's gun belt and buckled it to the rope. Together, that would be evidence enough for the court that Webb had died in the act of being served his warrant. Then, for himself and the young'uns, Bass dropped Webb's revolver down into one of the boots. Maybe it would be evidence enough for Bennie to be godly and follow rules, and he wouldn't want to grow up to leave his gun to a better man.

Since he didn't have a shovel for a proper burial, Bass kicked a veil of dirt over him and prayed Webb had found it in his heart, while it still beat, to accept Jesus there. He prayed he was planting a flower. By morning, after the cow killers and the coyotes, Webb's body would be unidentifiable.

He surveyed the carnage of Floyd's mare one last time, the blood spill as long and wide as a quilt. He remembered himself many years ago, when he was a different person, as if on a different planet, who could have been startled to distraction by the needless shooting of a horse. Webb had bet with his life that Bass had never changed.

Bass scooped up a handful of dirt and tossed it on the mare, a gesture for a friend, before easing back at a trot to Bywaters's Store.

◆ ◆ ◆

The store glowed with yellow lamplight in its darkly wooded alcove as if it contained a dying star. From across the clearing, Bass could hear Floyd speak in a speaking voice, not a mumbling or praying voice, but his words kept dragging too low to the ground to be made clear, even through the broken window. As if his words cast those shadows that flickered along the walls instead of normal meaning.

Bass slowed Strawberry to a walk and drew a pistol. The front door was now shut, but Webb's horses still stood at the yellowwood tree, batting their tails. The mound of Fringe at the edge of the clearing still appeared to breathe and twist in its same dying place it so teemed with white-faced possums chewing its flesh. Another horselike mound appeared at the end of the porch, with boots and clothes. Bywaters. A cub-sized coon, sixty pounds or more, sat on his chest, its mouth rooted deep in Bywaters's mouth.

A moan emanated from Bywaters's decomposing body, and the coon responded with a slurpy gurgle. The coon then withdrew its blood-covered snout to look at its feasting hole with raised ears.

Bass approached high enough on his perch to see Floyd sitting inside the store on Bywaters's stool with a bottle pressed to his mouth. He appeared alone.

The mound of Bywaters moaned again—a putrid, gassy thrum, chopped intermittently by what could have been the sticky passage of blood clots through a gnawed throat. Undeterred, the coon buried its snout back in Bywaters's mouth, and Bywaters grunted with more strength, as if, by God, he were yet alive.

Bass whistled a bobwhite song to announce himself, and a dog somewhere inside the store answered him with a string of young barks.

Floyd knocked the stool over getting off of it. "Goddog it, Bass!" He waved a pistol in his hand for Bass to join him, as if he knew Bass was somewhere beyond the window watching him.

Bass dismounted on tired legs and left Strawberry untied to feed on what grass there was.

Floyd flung the door open, and a white bulldog with a wagging tail clawed at the porch boards to reach Bass in the yard and smell him.

"Was beginning to worry this time," Floyd said, looking past Bass, toward Strawberry.

Bass offered the dog the back of his hand but held his Colt on it in case it gave him the slightest sense of being rabid.

Floyd groaned. "He got my mare?"

"He did," Bass said. The dog worked its tongue between his fingers and around his knuckles. "Just to be strange, I reckon. Shot it right out from under him like he thought anything he'd do would surprise me."

"Damn it, I liked that mare."

Bass lowered his head to get a good look at the pup, maybe a year old, licking like his salt would save it.

"What about Webb?" Floyd said.

"Had to leave him."

Floyd nodded and holstered his pistol. "Sometimes that's all they want."

"So where'd the pup come from?" Bass opened his hand to give up his palm.

"I couldn't tell you. Looked and there she was. A likable thing but don't know if I'd let her lick me." Floyd tipped his whiskey bottle toward her, as if Bass needed him to point the bitch out. "She probably lapped up a gallon of fat man's blood, until I hauled his ass out." He tipped the bottle in the direction of Bywaters. "Was beginning to stink something awful anyways." Floyd hitched his upper lip in a smirk of disgust and pulled a swallow.

Bass wiped his hand on his trousers. "You sure he ain't still alive?"

"Him? Been gone."

Bass stepped closer to Bywaters and rapped the porch with his Colt. The coon uprooted its snout to eye Bass. "Get!" he said, rapping the porch again, and the coon leaped off Bywaters, ducking into the shadows of the woods, and the white pup darted after it.

"Doornails don't move," Floyd said.

"Listen," Bass said.

They waited. The pup barked, then rustled back into the light, taking the porch steps and sniffing up the blood trail and licking it. A ghostly moan emanated from Bywaters's still body, then choked off.

Bass stepped to the porch's edge, close enough to see the full display of the man's blown-off face, like a fresh pan of turtle meat. "You hear me, Bywaters? This is Deputy Bass Reeves. You dying and that can't be helped."

"Jesus, Bass," Floyd whispered. "I thought the fat man was dead."

Bass leaned forward a little more and placed a hand on Bywaters's wet shoulder. "Time to start over is right now, Bywaters. Time to be somebody totally else." Bass patted him, and Bywaters emitted a slow-rising hiss. "You know what the devil will give you. Time to pray for what the Lord can give. Renew yourself, Bywaters. Make a clean slate."

"He almost there," Floyd said.

"That's right," Bass said. "You almost there." He patted Bywaters once more, that solid unmoving mound, as if his body had long been dead, had even begun to harden up, while his soul had hunkered down deep, afraid to come out.

Bass turned to the pup and offered her his hand. He holstered his Colt and turned to Floyd, who was plugging his bottle young'un-like with his finger. "I see you found some whiskey."

"Didn't have to look hard." He freed his finger from the bottle with a pop. "Come see for yourself." Floyd turned and shuffled inside. "Like a damn waterfall of it."

June bugs clung to the porch walls and crunched beneath Bass's boots as he took the steps. His legs heavy as tombstones. The pup ran ahead of him, following the long, dried smear of blood that Floyd followed himself, as if they'd all lost their way and needed a path to follow. Any at all.

Floyd grabbed the lamp on the way through and showed Bass the storeroom of whiskey, hay-stuffed crates stacked to the rafters. They gazed at the work ahead of them, while Bass, more thirsty than hungry, ate a sour pickle from a barrel.

"You find any bookkeeping?"

Floyd shook his head and swilled his bottle dry.

"You look close?"

Floyd nodded and swapped the empty fifth for a new one, shedding bits of straw as it moved through the light.

"Bound to kept books," Bass said.

Floyd clamped down on the cork of the new bottle with his back teeth and wrenched it free. He handed Bass the bottle and lamp and took the cork from his mouth. "Watch this," he said. "She expects anything's food." He held the cork high above the pup, and the pup stood tall on her hind legs, begging for it, dancing. "Want it?" he said, bobbing the cork just out of her reach. "You want it, you want it, okay, get it," he said and tossed the cork over his shoulder. He laughed, watching the pup scamper after it.

Bass took a swig, ignoring Floyd's drunkenness, then set the bottle and the lamp on the lid of the pickle barrel and began loading his arms with bottles from the open crate and toting them outside to start a trash pile next to Bywaters. Hopefully, that would cut the smell some and scare the coon off.

He and Floyd worked for nearly an hour breaking open crates and breaking contraband and cutting smell. They'd stop to listen to Bywaters, but they hadn't heard anything else from him since the hiss. Maybe that was good. Maybe Bywaters had given up the ghost to God, but waiting for nothing to come around seemed sad, too, and close to a warning. Bass didn't like it.

The pup followed them back and forth, sometimes behind Floyd, sometimes Bass. Floyd stopped now and again to sip spared whiskey. Bass sipped too or ate a pickle.

"You look in the register or under it?" Bass asked.

"Yep. First place," Floyd said.

When they'd broken all they were going to break, Bass sighed and gestured at Bywaters. "Time for *him* now."

"I don't know," Floyd said. "Time for bed what I'm thinking."

"Be the right thing," Bass said, deciding to take off his coat and roll up his sleeves.

"Ain't you tired?" Floyd said.

"Been tired. Come on."

Bass took the lamp behind the store to find shovels and also a shed stocked with oats. He fed Strawberry and Webb's bays and watered them, while Floyd got to work on the grave.

Strawberry, not this one but the first one, had waited for Bass to return—ears up and whisking his tail beneath Ben Colbert's ferry rope, strung across the Red River from the Texas blackjack beside him to a free one beside Bass, as if Bass would one day cross back and live with him again. He didn't try to remember how that Strawberry had been different from this one. He guessed it had died long ago. His old master, not the son but the first one, the father, had died in June of 1872 at the age of seventy-eight. Jennie had spread the *Van Buren Press* across her lap and read the obituary aloud. Bass remembered crossing the parlor to see for himself, to look at the name, the first and only time he'd ever seen it: *William Steele Reeves.* He would find out later from a friend of a friend that the old master had died peacefully in bed one afternoon at his infernal son's house in Grayson County, Texas. He remembered that sinking sad feeling seeing the name in newspaper ink. The master had been the closest thing he had ever allowed Bass to have as a father. Bass couldn't help the feeling of mourning and didn't fight it. But as soon as Jennie tucked the folded newspaper away, Bass, as he recalled, had instantly felt differently about something that was different.

He peered over the hole. "Take you a rest," he told Floyd, and he finished the grave himself. Then he climbed out, and Floyd helped him roll the fat man in and cover him up.

Floyd jabbed the spade into the loose dirt of the grave and flopped down on the ground. "Damn tuckered, I'm tuckered," he said, reaching for the bottle standing on the porch's edge.

Bass offered the same words for Bywaters as he had for Webb hours earlier.

"I liked that mare, Bass. Was a damn good horse."

"Mine, too," Bass said, patting the pup now sitting beside him. "My boy'll miss him." He stood his spade in the dirt at an angle so that it made a cross with the other one. To loosen the crick in his neck, he leaned his head back and gazed at the sky's moonless flickering. Like a field of lightning bugs. Like nothing special like that. What was on God's mind, he wondered, to give him that to look at, at this instant, tired as he was, tired as Floyd was, as dead as so much was around them, as far off as his family was, asleep long ago?

"We gonna take those bays of Webb with us, ain't we?" Floyd asked. "Seeing as we owed and nobody's alive to tend to them anyway?"

"This time, I reckon," he said.

"The ornery cusser didn't leave us much choice."

"Before he died," Bass said, "he gave me his pistol and scabbard." He drew his eyes around the Big Dipper and Little Dipper. He usually thought of them as rainbows, promises of that permanent station you got up high when you drank from the Lord. Tonight, this moment, he saw scabbards.

"He'd want you to have his horses, too, sounds to me," Floyd said. He tossed his empty bottle onto the pile of empties on the other side of the grave.

Bass stroked the velvet fur across the pup's broad head and folded ears, and kicked Floyd's boot. "We best catch a quick shut-eye before heading back."

"There's a bed and cot in back there."

"I expect so," Bass said. He staggered from exhaustion as he meandered through the store, checking this place and that place tucked behind canned meat or medicine bottles, under belts of fabric.

"I checked there," Floyd said, this place and that. "There, too," he said.

Eventually there was nowhere else to look for a record book but in the bedroom.

"Look in here?" Bass asked.

"Here, too," Floyd said.

The lamp in Bass's hand cast a rounded yellow pall over the cot pitched in immediate reach, the coat rolled up for a pillow, the taller cast-iron bed with actual pillows, the washbasin between the bed and cot, and the hat hanging from a hook above it. The pup hopped onto the cot and circled before lying down.

"This'll do me," Floyd said, falling in with the pup with his boots hanging over the end of the cot. Bass stepped around Floyd's boots, gummed with mud like his own, and held the lamp higher. Above the bed hung a framed picture of a ship rocking somewhere at sea. He leaned in to examine the white-crested waves for a fin or the spray of a whale. He doubted he'd ever see a sea or whale in his lifetime. His eyes trailed the wake of the ship to the ship itself and looked for people on board, Black or white, for anyone thrown overboard. But it was just a painting of a ship tossed at sea.

The lamp failed to light the corners of the room, until he stretched his arm over the bed and saw there was nothing in the corners. Nothing under the mattress either, or under the pillows. Nothing at all to take back to Fort Smith to prove Bywaters had ever possessed motive to pose a threat. Only that jagged pile of bottles beside the man's grave. It was a good thing these days that there were white people like Judge Parker who trusted the word of a Negro or that of a Negro's hired hand. One day, though, with little notice, they might, like Negro Fort, like Spanish Florida, like so many people and places and things, all again be gone.

11

Tock Tock

Even though he felt heavy with fatigue, Bass could not sleep. Not in the sag of Bywaters's bed, next to Floyd snoring in Webb's cot, if that was Webb's cot, with Webb's pup's paw twitching like she was waving at him, if that was Webb's pup. Not with a hat hardly over his eyes with a cut brim. Not with the lamp still burning like a low fire because Floyd liked a fire in a strange place. Not with that empty ship forever tipped above him and that hat of his, with its cut brim. And not with the circuit preacher's widow he didn't know by name obsessively winding clocks at this hour, which his hat couldn't begin to shield—hearing her pace *tock tock* from clock to clock, or something like clocks. Not with that widow looking in his mind like Jennie.

Bass could always sleep when he chose, but now he couldn't. That's how God spoke to him, by breaking one of his gifts to show him he could. The widow was up and losing her faith, God was telling him, so he ought to be up, too.

Bass recalled the time a crate of oysters on ice arrived at the plantation in Van Buren with a skinny blue iris painted on its side. After Bass wrenched the lid free, Master Reeves let him watch as he split the oysters open and ate their fresh meat like a drink. Sometimes in the folds of muscle the master found a pearl—beautiful and white even if from the bottom of the sea. As white as cotton can be, even at night. Bass imagined the widow imagining her husband as a boy or young man witnessing the promise of oysters, thinking how hope could be found anywhere God was, and how it could also be taken away by any old white man hungering after it.

He gave Floyd's shoulder a hard shake. "Time to go."

Floyd groaned and slipped back to sleep, so Bass shook him again. "We got a telegram to send. Get up, Floyd. This ain't a good place. Let's get up from it, hear?"

Bass helped him stand, and the pup stretched and yawned.

"You take Strawberry," Bass said. Floyd's saddle was still strapped to him, but that wasn't all. Floyd could make a bed of the sorrel, with Strawberry's broad back and smoother gate, if Floyd was determined to.

The pup begged on hind legs to go up on Strawberry with him.

"You want to keep her?" Bass asked.

"Don't you?"

Bass leaned down and picked her up, the brightest thing under the sky, and set her on Floyd's lap.

Floyd muttered to her to be still, *Be still*, while Bass trudged across the clearing for his saddle resting a few feet from Fringe, who was motionless now himself, the possums having finally surrendered to the meal; only the stink stirred. Bass trudged back again to the yellowwood tree. He only needed one horse, but he fixed a tether rope for the other bay. He couldn't leave a thing stranded.

If it wouldn't have been considered a crime, he would've set that store ablaze, if not just to light their way better getting up the road.

◆ ◆ ◆

Not long after sunrise they found Willy sitting on Pearlalee's hominy, both sacks stacked to make a chair beside the campfire. He clutched his pistol in one hand and a coffeepot in the other.

"About time," Willy said. And then he jumped to his feet, aiming his Smith and Wesson at the wagging pup charging at him. "What's this? What's this?" he hollered.

"Don't you dare shoot her," Floyd said.

"Better get her then," Willy said.

"My goodness," Bass said, watching the pup back off from Willy and direct her nose toward the pan sizzling up something on a bed of embers.

Floyd caught up to her and grabbed her tail.

"Why don't you put your arm away before you hurt somebody," Bass said.

Willy leered at the pup, then turned his leer at Bass, and turned his revolver at Bass, too, almost as an accident as he swept it across his body and paused, before nosing it down into its scabbard. "Just keep her out of my breakfast. I ain't cooking for her, so don't ask me." He shifted his attention to what was in the pan and sat back down on Pearlalee's hominy. "Y'all's dog—y'all feed it."

Bass folded his arms and waited for Willy to look at him and see the brim on his hat was cut. He could survive a lot worse than what Willy could throw out. But Willy only stared at his pan or watched the coffee pour from the pot into his tin cup.

"You one a us or not?" he asked him. "Either you wanna know what we been through or you don't."

Willy set the pot in the fire and blew on his coffee. "I reckon with all that blood and mud and mess caked on the two a you, you killed who you was hunting and brought back they dog. Real sweet a you." He raised his eyes at Floyd. "That close?"

"You make it sound easy," Floyd said.

"Ain't it?" Willy stuck the point of a knife into the head of the catfish he was frying and turned it over.

Floyd made a quivering fart sound with his mouth, then stood up with the dog in his arms and looked at Bass. "Got time for a dip if I make it quick?"

Bass focused on Floyd for the first good time in a while, with the morning sun trickling through the leaf petals of the hickory trees and lighting on Floyd's cheeks and shoulders, giving Bass a just glimpse of their filth. The dog, in contrast, looked somehow brand-spanking new.

Bass tilted his head toward the lake. "Wouldn't hurt to give the pup a rinse off, too," he said and pulled an arm through a coat sleeve.

◆ ◆ ◆

The outfit arrived in Tishomingo at midday on the first of May. The Indian agency, where the Lighthorse police were stationed, was wired with a telegraph and holding four Creek prisoners to be transported to Fort Smith for larceny. A fifth prisoner was held nearby in the home of a doctor, a white man charged with attempted murder who was sick with dysentery. For a share of the bounties, Bass was happy to haul them.

Bass stood back in demonstration, with a hand resting on the handle of one of his holstered six-shooters, while Floyd began loading the Creek prisoners onto the wagon one at a time and locking the irons. The Indians climbed with dusty shoes or bare feet, and for the one without a shirt, his braids looked blacker. They sat in facing pairs but were as silent and sullen as captured slaves.

You been a poor mistreated folk, that's a fact, Bass thought, *but you about to be treated fair.*

The pup had danced on Floyd's wagon seat at the first sight of the newcomers but had settled across it and was sleepily panting.

Bass looked over his shoulder at Willy, sitting on his grub wagon seat, wielding his Smith and Wesson at the prisoners. Staring mad, hoping one would try something, you could see it.

"You one a us now?" Bass asked.

Willy continued to stare at the prisoners as if he were afraid if he looked away for an instant he might miss his chance to fire. "Who is *us*?" he said. "Lot a *us*es here."

"*Us* us."

"*Us us*?" Willy said. He didn't blink.

The time had finally come, Bass realized, for him to hire a new cook. For forty dollars a month, it wouldn't be hard. The going rate for cooks was half that, but he'd doubled Willy's pay, since Willy had agreed to assist Floyd with guard duty. Hiring a guard would've cost Bass three dollars a day, so the arrangement had worked out for everybody.

Bass watched Floyd hop down from the prisoner wagon and collect his shotgun lying on the ground at Bass's feet. "Come with me," Bass said. "I need your spelling."

They returned to the office, and Bass dictated two telegrams. He sent the first one to the court in Fort Smith:

I tracked Jim Webb to Arlin Bywaters Store in the Chickasaw Nation, I.T. Both are dead after shootout. Please send word to Rev William Steward's widow. Broke up some 20 gal. of whiskey Bywaters was seen selling out of store & confiscated two bay horses to complete duty since Webb killed two of mine. Advising investigation of Washington-McLish cattle drives as source of whiskey introduction. I remain

    Very Respectfully
    Bass Reeves
    Deputy U.S. Marshal

The second transmission went to the territorial newspaper *Indian Champion*, headquartered in Atoka, Choctaw Nation:

On April 30 fugitive on murder charge Jim Webb was found at Bywaters Store in the Chickasaw Nation, I.T. I defended myself when Webb a Mexican and Arlin Bywaters a white whiskey peddler refused to be served and began firing. I killed Bywaters with shotgun and pursued Webb who took flight on horseback after pinning me down. Shot at four times at close range but missed. A hearty chase ended north of the Arbuckles when I killed Webb with Winchester after his horse give out & he resumed firing. Bywaters can be found buried beside 20 gal. of broken glass. I am

    Yours Respectfully
    James Mershon
    Deputy U.S. Marshal

This wasn't the first time Bass had disguised events in the territory to confound adversaries, though his concern before had always been to keep his whereabouts concealed from those he was tracking. His intention this time was entirely different. Something told him, and it must have been God's voice, to keep the public from knowing just how many white men he was killing, which was why

Bass called Webb a Mexican without certainty of it. To keep hostility from festering into something against Negroes a court even the size of the Western District of Arkansas couldn't handle. If a Negro Fort nation were ever to happen, he had to proceed every moment to his last with the same caution he'd shown when creeping up easy-like on the Coldirons. There had never been much room for error for people still viewed as gourds, even in a gourd field.

Bass had never given James any warning whenever he'd used his name, and he wouldn't this time. It was much more fun for Bass to run into him at the courthouse and hear how James, in his Kentucky accent, had learned of the news. If he'd been caught off guard again by a reporter's question or if, like last time, cornered by his pastor after the service for the truth the paper couldn't print. To hear James tell in his wonderfully droll way what he'd made up from beginning to end, without ever cracking a smile, could double Bass over in a fit of laughter. Bass could cry and hurt in his gut from it. James knew how to get him back.

◆ ◆ ◆

Bass and Floyd walked to the end of the block, at the edge of town, where the doctor's house faced them with the kind of pretty trim along the eaves and porch rails that Bass hadn't the talent to duplicate for his showplace. He sure liked it and could afford it, but if he couldn't build it himself, he wouldn't have it.

They strode up to the front door, and Bass knocked as they stomped dust from their boots.

The doctor opened the door wearing a stethoscope around his neck, a cute Cooper Double-Action holstered on his hip, and a gold pocket watch on a vest chain.

"How do?" Bass said.

The doctor's eyes met Bass on Bass's badge. "Deputy," he said, taking a step back and leading them in to the prisoner, Lamar Grayson, who smelled there on a bed in the parlor like the inside of a goat. His teenage wife, Mary, sat by his side. Right off, she let Bass know she expected to travel with her husband.

"You ain't got young'uns?" Bass asked.

"I ain't got nothing," she said.

"Well," Bass said, "we ain't going to Fort Smith directly. Might be weeks before we aim there. I ain't got an idea."

"We ain't in no hurry."

He smiled at her. She was sweet. "You think that now before you sit a month in the sun in my wagon, and I gotta fill my wagon, make my money first, you understand?"

She nodded. "I'll help out any way I can—cook or wash or whatnot, whatever you please," she said, without even a bag. With just a worn old dress hanging on her shoulders and a husband with the shits.

"Gonna have to lift that dress for me," Bass said.

"Whatever it takes," she said, but didn't move.

"I mean now," he said.

Mary Grayson consulted the doctor.

"This is the law, silly girl," the doctor told her. "Do what he says if you're determined to go along."

The girl glanced at Floyd before looking again at Bass. She scrunched her face and her thick black eyebrows became one. "Right here?"

"Well, yeah, right here," Bass said. "Before you step a foot in my wagon."

Mary stood up from her husband's bed and lay down on the floor.

"Not that way," Bass told her.

Floyd and the doctor gave each other a look and snickered.

Bass reached out a hand to help her up. "Just show me you ain't hiding a weapon."

"Oh," she said, and she grabbed onto his thumb, not his hand, and sprang herself up onto her toes with the easy motion of a whirligig and immediately hiked her dress up to her waist, showing she owned nothing beneath it either, no bloomers or garters, just the pale skin she was born with and a thicket so dense Bass had a mind to run his fingers through it just to be safe. Mary turned herself around and let her dress fall. "See, I ain't hiding nothing," she said.

"Perty, huh?" her husband said. "Show 'em again, Mary."

"Nah, now," Bass said, catching her arm before she showed herself again. "I reckon we seen enough."

The doctor turned away and returned with a package wrapped in paper and bound with twine. "Make sure Mr. Grayson gets plenty of water throughout the day," he told Bass. He gave the package to Mary. "And two or three times a day he needs a strong cup of tea from this cottonwood bark." He looked from Mary to Bass, and they both agreed with a nod of the head. Then Bass took the package from Mary. He untied the twine and unfolded the paper. Cottonwood bark, sure enough. "Sorry," he told the doctor.

"No, do your job," the doctor said.

Bass handed the loose bundle to Mary. "Sorry, ma'am." He waved Floyd over, and they collected her husband by the arms and legs and carried him down the street to the wagon. They crowded him at the Creek prisoners' feet, and while Floyd shackled Lamar Grayson's ankles, Bass helped Mary into the wagon and onto a bench seat beside one of the Creeks, with the bark a tidy package again, proud as a birthday present in her lap.

Bass mounted Strawberry, and Floyd climbed to his wagon seat.

"Hey, boss," Floyd said, the pup sitting perky beside him, "some tumbleweed back there, huh?"

Bass chuckled. "Yes, indeed. A tumbleweed in the Tumbleweed! That's a first."

"Ha!" Floyd said.

"What you two yahoos yammering about?" Willy asked from his own wagon seat, his Smith and Wesson finally put away.

"Nothing," Bass said. "Ain't hiding nothing, right, Floyd?"

Floyd tried to laugh silently but lost it, and then Bass lost it with him. It didn't seem they would ever regain their composure, and when finally they'd gathered themselves, Lamar Grayson farted and that riled the pup to barking, sending Bass and Floyd right back to the beginning.

"It's not funny!" Mary said. "He can't help it."

"That's them," Willy said.

"Sorry, ma'am," Bass said. He knew he shouldn't laugh, but whenever the pup finally showed signs of settling down, Lamar Grayson would fart again and rile the pup, and that would tickle Bass or tickle Floyd and they'd both go back to belly-laughing. Even the Creeks joined in, and they weren't famous for their humor. It got to a point that it wasn't even funny anymore to Bass, but he couldn't stop—until the goat smell of the farts began to float his way and he knew he needed to get moving quick.

12

A Deeper Darkness

Rain clouds drifted in scabs and Bass fired, click-clacked, and fired, and out of the smoke of his Winchester he re-saw Webb fall backward, as if the cloud of smoke itself, a cloud like these, had pulled the trigger. As if only white could defeat white. He didn't know why his thoughts drifted back to Webb, who'd drifted closer to him in the end, as the hunter and hunted will, calling him brave despite calling him a n——, and giving him his pistol and scabbard, or why men, like cattle, roamed back and forth over the land between us in the first place, or why one thing ever looked like another and made a body wonder.

They were following a stage road northwest toward Cherokee Town. About two miles out, Bass led his outfit down the sunken depression of an old cattle trail that crossed northeastward to a spot of green he remembered from two years earlier, in 1882, when he had to give Strawberry a rest after a hard race with Hellubee Sammy, the cinnamon-colored son of a Creek freedman who was riding a fine ink-black colt of a large but elegant breed Bass had never seen before—with tiny ears and a rounded neck and flowing mane and tail, crimped like a woman's. Bass had tethered the colt to Strawberry and was leading Hellubee, his prisoner, back to his camp not far from White Bead Hill. Hellubee bragged for miles that his horse could beat Bass's in a race and begged to let him prove it.

"Who'd you steal him from?" Bass asked with his eyes on the road ahead of him. It was late in the day and Bass was thirsty.

"That don't matter," Hellubee said. "What matters is I ain't got the horse you arresting me for. You might as well go ahead and let me go now without it. But if I gotta deal for you to do the right thing, then let's race for it. If I win, like I know I will, then I'm free. I'm gone. What do you say, deputy? It'll be fun. It'll do your old blood good to game some, too. You know it will."

Bass had a mind to teach the cocksure boy a lesson. And he was curious to see the colt run. "What is it?" Bass knew it wasn't a Morgan, what his old master, not the first one, the father, but the second one, the son, George Reeves, rode during the war, but that was all Bass could compare it to, as black as it was, though this one with the crimped hair was larger and prettier, a black dream with no white on it.

"What is what?" Hellubee asked.

Bass turned in his saddle. "The colt!"

"Oh, you wanna know what he is?" Hellubee grinned, showing he was missing teeth already at his young age of twenty-something. "He's a grown-man horse all I know—not an old-man horse like yours. He might dress like he likes a fuss because he does, because he's faster than the wind, I can tell you that. You caught me sleeping, deputy. You won't catch me riding. Come on, let's give it a go right now. You ain't got me with the right horse no-ways."

Bass halted Strawberry and watched the colt drift up beside him, a little longer and a little taller. "Look, I get paid the same turning you over whether your charges get dropped or not." He reached for his rifle and saw Hellubee's eyes grow twice in size. Then Bass shifted his hand to his saddle rider and produced the key to the irons on Hellubee's wrists.

Hellubee folded over with relief. "Whew," he said, suddenly giddy, "but you'll wish you'd shot me when I'm long gone from here." Then his face fell and he stiffened. "You ain't gonna shoot me, say I was running from you?"

Bass shook his head. "Bargain's a bargain." He unlocked the irons from Hellubee's wrists, and Hellubee groaned from relief. "Strawberry may not look like much," Bass told him, dropping the irons and the key back into his saddle rider, "but if we don't catch you, then you're free cause the Lord must want you free, and you will owe it to him to find out what it is you owe, hear? But if we beat you, then you ain't free, and you gotta lead me to the horse you stole and to the rich soul you snatched this colt from, too. Deal?"

Hellubee stopped rubbing his wrists and shot a hand out. "Let's do it," he said.

Bass shook his hand, then they tried to agree on a point in the future to run to. The boy aimed to make it a short race—this tree or that, fifty to a hundred yards away—because that was to his younger horse's advantage, but Bass insisted on giving Strawberry a fighting chance.

"Let's reach a place worth reaching," Bass said. "Sand Creek's about a mile from here. They'll need a treat."

Hellubee removed his dusty hat and wiped his dusty sleeve across his forehead. He wagged his head. "Don't matter," he said.

Bass untied the tether rope and looped it around the saddle horn, then unholstered a pistol to start the race. The crack might spook the colt but not Strawberry.

Hellubee fingered the reins until Bass was ready. Hellubee had the stirrups pulled high the way most Indians rode, so his elbows rested on his knees.

"Get ready," Bass said. He stroked Strawberry's neck, then made him dance in place the way Hellubee was winding up the colt.

By the colt's first leap, it was clear to Bass that Strawberry was never going to catch him. Bass let Strawberry do his best, then slowed him to a trot so he could watch that beautiful creature fly through the water and over the rocks and clover banks, to watch the spectacle of that black flag tail fly.

◆ ◆ ◆

Bass would dress in tramp clothes in the morning and ride Strawberry to the post office to have a word with the postmaster, along with a few others Bass knew. Chub Moore had been known to camp in a tight spot with his gang just outside of Cherokee Town, toward Johnsonville. Maybe he was there again.

Though the air didn't smell enough like rain yet, Bass and Floyd pitched the prisoner tent. Bass hammered stakes almost dreamily to the rhythm of *1-2-3 Save Jesus*. As tired as he was, he could slip off into a different time and hear Uncle Moseley in the field leading slaves to song, as if Uncle Moseley were in front of him somewhere he wasn't looking, in the night's first shadows. As if Willy, behind him, bearing his pistol over the prisoners, were an overseer—just as limp with boredom and just as mad about it.

Once the tent was tied up, Bass and Floyd carried Lamar Grayson to the creek and let his wife wash him off while they began moving the other prisoners under the tent and shackling them together and then all of them to a chain that wrapped around the axle of the prisoner wagon.

After Willy got the fire started, he stacked up Pearlalee's hominy and sat. Bass didn't much mind, but he wouldn't have minded one lick if Willy had at least asked if he could plant his bottom on his mother's morning meal. Willy occasionally stoked the fire with a long hickory branch he'd whittled smooth during his time by the lake. Waiting for a pot of water to boil for Lamar Grayson's cottonwood tea, Willy hardly stirred from his seat on the stacked hominy, stoking the fire with his stoking stick or sipping creek water from his cup or turning his head to gaze off at Mary, wherever she was, bending over her husband. Once Lamar Grayson was washed off and chained to the rest of the prisoners, Mary, like the moon tonight, hid herself away, and Willy put on a pan of salt pork and a pot of beans.

Bass was telling Floyd what he knew of Chub Moore, and about the times he'd come close but not close enough to capturing the Chickasaw suspect over the years. They sat on their bedrolls, against their saddles.

"So did the Negro he lynched rape that woman?" Floyd asked, holding the pup in his lap as much as petting her—her nose working at the smell of fried pork.

Bass hunched his shoulders. "Woman said he did."

"Then I guess, by damn, n—— did if the white woman say so," Willy said, jabbing the fire with his stick and eyeing the fire as if he were also talking to the fire.

Bass hunched his shoulders. "Maybe did. Maybe didn't. Don't much matter."

"Don't much matter?" Willy said.

"Would you make up some corn pone to go with those beans, Willy?" Floyd asked. "Corn pone sounds good with beans and pork, don't it to you, too, Bass?"

For an instant, Willy stared through the heat waves and smoke trickles over the fire directly at Bass, then turned to Floyd, seated closer, but not directly at him, more at the pup. "Corn pone for who?"

"For *who*?" Floyd stiffened. "For who wants it! What do you mean?"

"Not for the varmint but for you, maybe," Willy said. "Which is it?"

"Why not for the varmint?" Bass asked. "Why things mattering so much to you all of a sudden? What's got into you?"

"Look, I told y'all I ain't cooking for no mongrel." Willy leaned toward the fire and picked up a fork. "You wanna take over my business, then you do like you do." He looked toward Bass this time but not exactly at him.

Bass and Floyd eyed each other, but neither seemed to know what to think. Willy turned the pork over in a roar of grease.

Floyd turned to his saddle. "Never you mind then, Willy." He unbuckled a saddle rider. "I got some hardtack left. Just wanting something fresh."

"You got something to say?" Bass asked.

Willy scooted the pork. Stared at the pork.

"I do like I do?" Bass asked.

Willy nodded and scooted the pork again. "That right."

"What's right?"

"I mean what you know, Bass, about what matters with Negroes, what one did or didn't do to no white woman or why or whatever. You ain't no Negro like I ever knowed. That's what I mean. There."

Bass had a mind to let it go. He wiped his mustache from the corners of his mouth. "There where?" Bass said. He couldn't. "Best you free yourself. Time to be free, Willy. About time for it."

Willy twirled his fork in the air but stared down, his eyes beginning to bulge, as if he intended to scoot the pork with them. "You with your badge keeping the white man's law, you might as well be a bull in the ring, Bass Reeves."

"You the one with no neck," Bass said. Bass laughed and that invited Floyd to join in.

"I ain't messing," Willy said, scooting the pork now with his fork.

"Here," Floyd said, teasing the pup to stand on her hind legs for a piece of hardtack he held pinched high.

Bass decided this time to let it go and took up his rifle to clean it, remembering the dust of the whiskey trail, Webb's dust, and wanting none of it stored up like a ghost. He pulled out his knife from his coat pocket to remove the screws on the side plates.

"You don't scare me," Willy said.

"Hope not," Bass said. "Wasn't aiming to. My apologies if I did."

"Well, I said you didn't, damn it!"

Bass held up hands to say whoa, okay, sorry, but was too ornery to empty his hands first, bearing his knife and rifle.

Floyd laughed and teased the pup with another tear of tack.

"So you think I ain't Black cause you blacker, that it?" Bass asked.

Willy rolled his round head more than shook it. "Not a bit," he said. "You simply white through and through as your white daddy who taught you how to shoot is all."

Bass made a sound like laughter. He'd heard accusations like that before, back before his position as the master's body servant had won all the field slaves a load of gobbler meat at a turkey shoot, and after that he never heard it whispered again. "What makes you think my master was my daddy?"

"What makes you think he wasn't?"

Bass saw Willy sitting high and cracking a grin, sitting high and cracking a grin on his mother's hominy. "You gone perch yourself on my mama's hominy and call her a liar?"

Willy rolled his head. "I didn't call your mama no liar. *You* did." He laughed and curled his eyes at Floyd as if he expected Floyd to join in, but Floyd didn't. Floyd fed the pup a piece of tack and acted as though that was all that was going on.

Bass laid his rifle and his knife on the ground. He remembered a time when he'd wished Master Reeves had been his father, how it would've been a whole lot easier on everybody to have him that much closer. "Wouldn't much matter, would it?" he told Willy.

"There you go again," Willy said. "Everything like that matter. You'd know it if you was like me. You'd know it be long past time for no law atall for Black folks, like for Indian folks, and folks like you need to back your ass off sometime. Shore, arrest them white skins or, better still, shoot 'em dead, but leave everybody else the hell alone."

"To rape?" Bass asked.

"If want to."

"To kill, too?" Bass asked.

"Why not? Freedom's what we want, damn it, so give it to us a little while before you take it away again."

"So, why you out here with us, Willy?" Floyd asked.

"Closest I can get." He barreled his arms against his body and lowered his head. "Closest I can get."

"Shit, freedom it is then," Floyd said. He released the pup, and she dashed toward the pan with the pork.

"Get outta here, damn it!" Willy said, swinging a fist but missing her and then drawing his pistol.

"Put that away," Floyd hollered.

Bass whistled and the pup ran to him. He let her drink from his cup of water he was saving for his meal, and she lapped at it greedily. "Go check on 'em, will you, Floyd?" he said.

Floyd stalled in front of Willy, as if he was about to say something but thought better of it, and walked on to the prisoner tent. "How's he feeling?" Bass heard him say.

"You was just thirsty," Bass told the pup. "She was just thirsty," he told Willy.

Willy kept quiet, stewing over there on the other side of the fire. No high toss to the fire, the flames like easy waves on the Arkansas. Mary Grayson's voice carried over sweetly from the tent between cricket chirps. Bass missed a woman's voice. He stroked the dog's head and neck, and she lifted up her head with water streaming. He looked through the fire heat.

"Make some corn pone," Bass said. He gave the pup his fist, and she gnawed at his knuckles.

Willy stabbed the pork slab and slipped it into the pot of beans. He stirred the pot, then set his fork down and stood, holstering his pistol, flashing bright in the firelight.

Bass picked up his rifle, a dull thing but a good one, and gave the pup his hand again to let her gnaw and lick it, whatever she wanted. He watched Willy measure out cornmeal. After the war, Bass's father had moved to California for work and was never heard from again. Could be dead. Could be alive and remarried. Could be sailing on a ship somewhere, catching whales and spreading his seed all the way to China.

When the pup appeared to have forgotten all about the pork, Bass took his hand away to empty his rifle so he could clean it and could go on to sleep after he ate because he was still tired from yesterday. He click-clacked the lever to throw the cartridges, and the pup reached for the cartridge with her mouth as the first one popped free.

"Now, that's cute," Bass said. "Willy, watch this. Come on, watch this." He worked the lever again and the pup leaped to catch the thrown cartridge and was coming close. He gave the pup a pat and offered a smile to Willy, but Willy wasn't watching or wasn't watching anymore. "You don't think that be cute?"

Willy sat back down on Pearlalee's hominy. "I don't like varmints."

"Shit, Willy, you worrying if I'm Negro, but you got me worrying you ain't even human."

Floyd stepped back into the firelight. "You got a hungry crowd. I hope you almost done."

Bass watched for Willy's reaction, but Willy stewed on.

Floyd dropped down on his bedroll, and the pup ran to him and begged on hind legs.

"I ain't got no more tack, little pup," Floyd said. "You'll have to wait for old dawdler to finish dawdling."

Bass worked the lever again, waiting for the pup to run over to try to catch the cartridge, but she danced her way to the fire on her hind legs, begging from Willy.

Bass laughed. "You gone tell me that ain't cute? You human yet, Willy?"

Willy took a look at the pup, then split his lips into a smile through the heat, really at Bass this time, really a smile, too, then at Floyd. "All right," he said, reaching for the pan he'd cooked the pork in and taking it off the coals. He stuck his fork down in it.

"Come on, pup, open up," Willy said, standing to his feet to feed a dog, like this was *his* trick. Willy tapped the fork along the rim of the pan, and the pup danced closer, wagging her tail, her tongue lolling.

"Look at you," Floyd said.

"Look at me," Willy said. He held the pan over the pup's wide-open mouth, her lips pulled back and showing all of her teeth. He drew out an empty fork and twirled it near the pup's nose. "Smell good? Taste better," he said. He tipped the pan, and a rush of grease poured out in a heavy sizzle.

The pup tried to take it all, until she was all covered up with a white cloud of steam.

Bass jumped up as the pup fell backward like a human, writhing, hardly squealing, hardly gagging.

"Goddamn you," Floyd yelped. He took to his knees. "You killed her."

Bass and Floyd watched the pup convulse, while Willy nestled the pan back on the coals and tossed the fork in it.

"Goddamn you, Willy!" Floyd grabbed his hat off his head and slapped the ground with it. "Goddamn you!"

"That ain't right," Bass said.

"I told y'all I don't feed varmints. I told y'all to get that varmint from me. I told y'all." Willy bowed his shoulders while wiping his hands on his trousers and staring off into the trees. "Don't push me off my space or I'll commence to killing horses next." Then as if the thought had inspired him to act, Willy reached for the ivory grips of his pistol.

Bass raised his rifle in a fast aim from the waist to nick Willy in the meat of his neck, for what was hardly there—a stump, hardly a neck at all, more of a challenge than a body part—and fired.

Willy slapped at his neck and blood spurted through his fingers. His eyes rolled, and he fell forward into the fire.

"Whoa, oh shit, Bass," Floyd said. He stood up to look down. "You killed him. You killed Willy."

Bass strode around the fire, around Willy's squirming, and worked the lever. He lowered the barrel. That sweet pup was bleeding out, quivering. He pressed the muzzle to the cage around her heart and pulled the trigger. He turned to Willy and kicked him out of the embers, the spilled pot of beans, his clothes on fire, and he kicked it out.

"You all right," Bass told him, but he knew Willy wasn't. "Just a nick," he said, but he knew it wasn't. "Get up."

He waited but couldn't wait. Aggravated, he turned away, and his eyes found Strawberry's river-emptying blaze beyond the edge of light. Then, from the darkness, a deeper darkness emerged from the right and left, or left and right—those oily black eggs looking back.

As if Strawberry had been waiting all night, or longer, for this moment of need, he walked toward him, nodding into the light, into the wreckage, as if to carry him quickly out of it, along a path Bass could not yet see.

PART THREE

AFTER

13

A Wake

"Where you off to?" Floyd asked. As if Bass wouldn't have told him.

With a fist of mane Bass spun Strawberry around to see Floyd's bulged eyes in the fire's thin light. The scattered logs threw even less light on Willy, laid out between the men in a barrel hump on a rug of blood and beans. Where was he off to? And then he remembered. "To get old man Nat, I reckon." He knew he should at least do that.

"You sure I shouldn't and you stay?"

Bass groaned a no with closed lips because Nat could be a hard one to find.

Floyd leaned over Willy, who was too low in the tumbled shadows for Bass to see clearly. Willy's clothes still smoked. Bass could see that. And he could see Willy's legs were as still and straight as oars.

"Souse a rag and hold it to his neck. Clean him off some. Maybe he'll hold on."

Floyd looked up at Bass and just looked. "How, Bass?"

"You really gonna ask me that? After Bywaters?"

Floyd turned again to Willy and bent lower, reaching and maybe touching Willy, maybe searching for a pulse. Bass's eyes trailed away to what looked in the mess like a bloody tooth. It was too large to be one, so Bass gazed, trying to decipher its shape and hidden color, until the finer lines revealed themselves, the grooved spinner, the stick-like barrel that wasn't a stick at all. Bass hated the thing.

Floyd shook his head. "How, Bass?"

"Maybe that stubborn mule's stubborn yet, Floyd, and will hang on for Nat. Might for Nat. Gotta hurry." Bass thought he should slow down first and say a prayer but then he clicked like he couldn't help clicking, and Strawberry leaped away like he couldn't help leaping, wanting so badly to ride Bass bare back again, even on a packed-hard cattle trail, maybe especially so because Strawberry, with a belly full of clover, could now race away.

Bass found himself lost among the things they passed, as if his mind had a mind of its own to ride those shapes back to where Willy lay in the scattered fire, where Floyd was maybe saying a prayer or maybe wasn't. Bass should have stayed to bless him. He'd never been too angry to bless a body. His bullet had struck the meat of Willy's neck too deep, when he'd meant only to nick it. He didn't understand, mad or not, how he'd missed and sprung an artery. Willy had reached for the ivories, but before that he'd killed the white bull pup as if only because it was white, and the horses were next, he'd said, and had reached, as if Bass would allow it.

Bass had aimed his Winchester straight, right to the touch of Willy's neck, stumpy or not, because he hadn't wanted to kill him unless he had to. He'd wanted him alive, like he'd wanted Master Reeves, the son, alive, and Sean Hagan, the overseer. He'd wanted to change Willy's heart, meaning only to free a little blood to release the devil that could pour out a heavy pan with a heavy sizzle on a hungry begging pup. How that white pup, Webb's pup maybe, had fallen backward from that white cloud had been how Webb had fallen, that human. But Bass should have stayed to bless him before leaving. He should've, in case Floyd wouldn't and Willy couldn't wait.

When the tight trail through the saplings showed, they took the whipping through it and climbed the dirt-over-rock mound and were on the stage road to Cherokee Town and old man Nat. But once Strawberry had found his pace again, Bass had to slow him for the two creeks coming.

All Bass could reason was that he and Webb had had that long chase in the Arbuckles and then he and Floyd had dug a hole for Bywaters, and he hadn't slept good afterward because God had broken his sleep to show him he could, and then God had broken his aim to show him he could break any gift he'd ever given. On the moonless wind he could see Bywaters's picture of the ship rocking somewhere at sea, as if rocking for him on the first creek that came slipping up, with the dark sky of that painting hanging sure enough above it. Rocking like Strawberry was rocking, and it made Bass mad to see it. Of course, he couldn't have slept in Bywaters's bed with a picture like that hanging above him, as if Master Reeves had hammered it up there himself. As if Master Reeves had known all along that his runaway slave, who wasn't really his because Bass was still his daddy's, would wander up one day in the Chickasaw Nation and need some sleep after killing a killer and digging a hole, and would look up as he did and wonder if there was of all things a whale among the waves, if a tail or a hole or a case was somewhere indicating itself.

Bass hiked his boots around Strawberry's neck and let Strawberry cross where he remembered to cross. Strawberry waded in up to his knees, and the stoic white face of a barn owl sailed toward them as if patrolling over the length of the water. Once upon them, the owl turned upward and disappeared among the stars and the black airy nothing between them, or in the trees on the other bank.

Bass didn't like walking through so much memory, but he kept on as Strawberry walked, steadied, waded, and walked. He let himself remember how he'd finally spoken up to the master, calling him out as a cheat, and how the master had reached, how he'd whirled out of his chair for the ivories on his desk and knocked over a glass of rye and how that had splashed on Bass's feet, where he could still feel it, and not only because creek water was splashing his legs and arms now. He allowed himself to think it through once more, from so long ago.

How the master's jaws had slacked and his red pipe had dropped down like a bird pecking seed. How ivory-white, steam-white, pup- and barn-owl-white the grips of his Colt Dragoon had been before Bass struck him twice, and Mr. Hagan once. How he'd killed the patrollers and that kid and rode off like this.

◆ ◆ ◆

The woman Nat lived with said he wasn't back yet from seeing a man who'd lost half a hand to a hog. She stepped out on her porch and with the barrel of her shotgun pointed the way.

Bass thanked her and followed the road as if heading to Bear Creek but took a left at the first fork and a path on the right just past an outcropping of chittamwood. When the path came upon shacks crawling together like ants, he began watching for Nat's wagon, hitched to two hinnies.

Nat was the only man Bass had ever known to prefer hinnies to mules or donkeys or even horses, as if he liked his animals to look as shaggy about the head as he looked.

A door to one of the shacks opened without a sound, and a shadowed face watched Bass pass and tip his hat. Some doors already stood open, even though there was no breeze to speak of. Just a lingering hot breath buzzing with insects, while a hog snorted out of sight in its sleep.

He found the hinnies deep in, at the only shack showing candlelight. Sackcloth hung over paneless windows and the door was shut, as if to dampen the groans of the man inside. The hinnies roused with a start as if they were old like Nat, too, and only now heard Strawberry walking up.

Bass climbed down and felt tired and sore doing so. He hadn't slept much for too long of a stretch, that was true, and it would only get truer. The sackcloth at one of the windows waved from movement inside.

Bass planted a foot on a weak board and then on another as he slouched across the porch, believing the door would open any moment for him, but it didn't. He listened to Nat saying behind it, "Best chomp down on this, now. Come on, open up them chompers."

A man was sucking and blowing through teeth. Bass waited, and when the man quit, Nat said inside, "That's it. Now stay chomped."

Bass rapped on the thin door, and someone barefoot padded over to it and unlatched it. A Chickasaw woman looked out with a grim expression and saw his badge.

"Halito," Bass said, and the woman backed away solemnly, as if she had no choice before the law.

He swept his hat off his head and took a step. Candlelight waved over Nat, stooped in the center of the room over a man seated at a table with a belt between his teeth, until the woman shut the door behind Bass, and the light waved elsewhere.

The man's arm was laid across the table and tied down by rope. Nat held a hatchet by his side. "I need you be still as can be, you hear?"

The man nodded. The man heard. He just couldn't see. His hair was stringy with sweat and hung in his eyes, but his eyes looked squeezed tight, while he continued to suck air and groan out even around his chomp.

Nat turned and when he recognized Bass he walked his way. "Bazz," he said.

Bass tipped his head. "Nat."

Nat switched the hatchet to his left hand so they could shake. "Got a warrant for him?" He tried to look up at Bass but his curved back wouldn't let him.

"No, my cook has got shot in the neck. Not looking good, Nat. Need your help quick back at camp when you're done."

Nat nodded. "Gotta finish."

"Course," Bass said. "Got business I could tend to while I wait, if you think it'll be a bit."

Nat nodded. The moles on his cheeks and nose cast shadows. "Gonna be a bit."

Bass leaned in to speak lower. "Good time as any to pick up Chub Moore, I reckon."

Nat grimaced with few teeth. He took a step back and eyed Bass. "You going it alone?"

"I never mind trying. Word I hear is he's camped again in a tight spot with his gang out toward Johnsonville. That close, you know?"

Nat turned his face down and patted a foot. "I seen him but not there." He shook his head. "He shacked with a girl with a sick young'un. But if you come back with him and he see me, he'll know I told. Can't have that."

Bass watched the woman ease down to the floor and slide a basin beneath the table. Then she stood, and from the seat of one of the other chairs at the table she took up a man's shirt and a needle and spool and sat down.

Bass rested his hands on his hips and regarded Nat without blinking. "What if I make sure he can't see?"

"Like poke his eyes out?"

"Nah, like hood him."

"Like he dead?"

"Why not?"

Nat shrugged. "That girl a his will still see."

"See what?"

Nat chewed his bottom lip. "Maybe if you hood her or scare her good about keeping quiet, you think?"

"If need be."

"You wanting him for lynching that colored boy or something new?"

"For the boy."

Nat nodded. He raised the hatchet and pointed the blade to the west. "There a hog pen outside here."

Bass nodded.

Nat lowered the hatchet. "He in the shack on yonder side of it."

Bass turned to the woman, looking blind to hearing. Darning like there was nothing but darning to do. The man across from her just sucked air and chomped like there was nothing else either. Bass looked back at Nat.

"I didn't say nothing about nothing," Nat said. "Shoot, I gotta hand to lop. Gonna be a bit though."

Bass walked toward the door, and the sackcloth draperies billowed like gills. He stopped at the door and turned to watch Nat sawing the hatchet blade in and out of the candle flame. Nat spoke to the man but Bass wasn't listening. He was watching Nat and then the woman as she pushed and pulled her needle without a flinch, even as Nat reared back and whacked the table.

The candle fluttered nearly out as the man choked and bucked until his ears turned red. Blood pooled and ran off one side of the table onto the floor, and the woman nudged the basin with her foot to catch it.

Bass backed out of the shack and shut the door. He smelled the hogs before he saw them. A sow and six piglets lay bumped against each other in one pen, while two boars slept apart in another. The sow and boars snorted without really stirring, as if only to smell Bass to remember him.

The ground outside the pens was soft as the mud appeared inside them. A horse was tacked and tied outside to a porch post. It could have been Chub's horse and Chub's rope Bass was taking into his own hands and carrying to the door.

The door wasn't locked so Bass walked in. A boy wheezed in his sleep in a bed next to a stove. A man snored in a bed across the room and a girl slept with him. The lamp on the table wasn't lit so Bass lit it.

The girl's eyes flashed open but not the man's, and she didn't move to wake him.

Bass walked closer, raising and aiming his Colt at her. With his other hand he tapped his badge, for her to see it, too. "Chub Moore?" he asked in a whisper.

She didn't answer so he repeated himself, and this time she squeezed her eyes shut and nodded.

He nudged her arm and when her eyes opened again, he pointed toward her son.

She seemed to understand. She drew her blanket aside and crossed the room to bend down next to him.

Bass walked around the bed, avoiding trousers, pistols, and boots in a heap. Against the wall leaned a rifle and a shotgun. Bass debated what to do. Knocking Chub out while he was already out seemed so much simpler. Since God was gracing him again, he wouldn't.

He shook Chub's arm, and Chub tried to gulp his snoring and then woke with a start.

Bass cocked the hammer back to give him proof the situation was serious. Chub's eyes went round, and Bass pressed the nose of the barrel against his cheek.

"Chub Moore, I'm Deputy Marshal Bass Reeves. I gotta writ with your name on it I been carrying a long time to show you. A long, long time. I want you to turn over so I can tie your hands, you understand me?"

Chub grunted and his eyes darted away from Bass.

"I expect you want to fight but no use fighting this time, Chub. Ain't no cabbage feast tonight. We got numbers. It's over. Turn over." Bass pulled the Colt away to give him room. "You hear me?"

Chub grunted again but turned over. And then he flipped back onto his back and thrashed his arms and legs at Bass and the Colt in his hand.

Bass jumped back, letting him thrash, and then swung down fiercely, buffaloing Chub high in the cheek with the barrel of his Colt. Then twice more to knock him out.

Bass looked back at the girl, startled but staying put.

"English?"

She cried but nodded.

He holstered his pistol and began tying Chub's hands together. When he finished, he cut off the slack end of the rope and walked over to the girl. "I almost got a mind to take you in for hiding a fugitive, you got me?" Instead, he tied her hands to the stove door and stood up.

The boy slept on like a boy will.

"I'll have somebody come cut you loose in a bit," Bass said. "Not before I get down the road, but in a bit, you hear?"

Her body shook but she nodded.

Bass saw a cloth wrapped around a pot handle and tugged it free. He walked back to Chub and tied it tight around Chub's head to cover his eyes. Then he hooked an arm through Chub's tied hands and dragged him off the bed and across the room.

"I'll tell a neighbor to come by in a bit, you hear?"

She nodded but continued to cry.

Bass felt bad about tying her up. About taking her cloth. Her pot handle would get mighty hot without it. If he wasn't without his saddle and his saddle rider and his coin purse and the silver inside it, he'd just bring her back a dollar.

14

A Tail

Nat stopped at the edge of Willy's pool of shadows and studied him from there, as if he wanted no closer. Bass pulled a stick from Floyd's remade fire and stepped up beside Nat and saw finally what Nat saw.

"He didn't look this dead before."

Nat groaned displeasure and walked easy-like the rest of the way over the slippery, spilled mess. He inched down on his haunches and placed a hand on Willy's chest and shook him, then reached for Willy's hand and held it.

"I cleaned his neck best I could," Floyd said. He sat on the two sacks of Pearlalee's hominy on the other side of the fire. "Said a prayer, too. A good'un."

Nat let go of Willy's hand and leaned over Willy's short neck, waving flies off the wound. Bass blew on the embers and held the stick close to it. The wound gaped like a dead open mouth. The severed artery like two baby ones. The blood droplets from the amputation looked on Nat's arm in the firelight like strewn feed.

Nat groaned again, then pushed on his knees to rise. He steadied himself and stretched his back before turning. "Even if I was home and ready for you, I couldn't a done nothing here. Even if I was here when it happened. Just so's you know."

Bass gave him a pat on his rounded shoulders. "Thanks for coming, Nat."

"Two dollars for coming," Nat said.

"Thanks all the same," Bass said. He smiled flatly, and Nat shook his head.

"You did what you could. I did what I could. Some things be perfect that way. Can't be helped." Nat wiped his hands on his trousers as he walked back to his wagon.

Bass retrieved two dollars and paid him, then to the rhythm of Nat's hinnies hoofing away, he and Floyd carried Chub Moore, still limp, to the prisoner tent, where they chained him and untied his blindfold.

Mary Grayson opened her eyes. Her hands were balled childlike at her face. "Hey," she said in a low, sweet way.

"Ma'am?" Bass said.

She unballed her hands. "How's the cook faring?"

"Never you mind," Floyd said. "Go on to sleep. It's over."

"Accident," Bass said to her. "Bad accident." He trudged back to their new campfire, not far from the old one, which wasn't far from Willy. "I see you hauled the pup off."

"Buried her."

Bass nodded. "Time for Willy now."

"I reckon."

Bass gazed at Willy's pool and the pup's pool, at the debris of leaves and ash and pots and pans and beans and that infernal Smith and Wesson, which all appeared to float there without movement as if in a painting.

"I hate he went," Bass said.

"Me, too. He had no right to kill my pup, though."

"No."

"Or threaten to kill nothing else."

"I agree."

"I mean, he reached."

"He reached," Bass agreed. Willy had sucked in his gut and there was the flash of white like light—the ivories, the smoke, the blaze, nearly all at once.

"Remember how you was cleaning your gun?"

Bass looked away, toward the prisoner tent. It glowed like a shelf of snow, like an officers' tent. "Was about to," Bass said. "I was emptying it to clean it."

"Bad accidents happen."

Bass looked at Floyd to read his eyes. "Sometimes."

"What you gonna say, Bass?"

Bass blinked. What else? "The truth."

"That's what I been thinking about all the time you was gone." Floyd reached into his coat pocket and drew out a leather pouch, then from the pouch a rope of tobacco. He looked at Bass as if to read his eyes and tore off a chew. His jaws popped as they worked to soften it. "Been thinking how you was cleaning your gun when Willy went and done his hateful thing." He put his pouch away and slipped his hands into his back pockets. "Been thinking how bad accidents happen like that, you know? You didn't mean to pull the trigger when you did, am I right, Bass? That's what happened, ain't it? A cartridge got jammed like they will and it went off? Something nobody could help?"

Bass leaned back, and then leaned in. "I aimed to nick him. Just to nick him. The accident, Floyd, was I just didn't. That's the truth. That's it." He turned toward the grub wagon. "Come on," he said.

He climbed up and found the spades. He handed one down to Floyd and hopped to the ground with the other.

"Nobody knows you to miss," Floyd said.

Bass looked around for the best place to dig and decided this was it, the mess of where Willy was, with his feet pointing eastward to the rising sun. He touched the blade to the old campfire ash and beans and blood but didn't start. "I miss," he said.

"When? You got a witness, boss? I ain't seen it."

"I didn't say a lot but course I have."

"But nobody knows you to. Now suddenly you do? That's all I'm saying."

Bass hung his boot on the spade's shoulder and ripped the earth as if it were a shirt. "People also know me to tell the truth, don't they?" He tossed the dirt, or tried to. The topsoil was soaked as if from a rain and clung to the spade. He had to shake it off, in dark clumps; then he stuck the spade back into the earth. He was glad a spade was a rigid thing, like a knife, a rifle, a hammer, like tongs, like an oar. But not like tongs, really. Like a post rather, or a yoke, a plow. Some things needed to be.

Floyd spat and stood his spade up on the western end of the grave. "You right," he said. "Till something happens. But you right."

◆ ◆ ◆

Bass shouldn't have found himself awake at such a dark hour this late or this early, and he shouldn't have been hauling himself up, not with so much sleep he was owed. He was getting ahead of himself to want to be on the road, he knew, but he couldn't lie still any longer, not with Willy in the ground and no one in Fort Smith or Van Buren knowing it. It was important for him to get his side out before people talked and made one up.

But he was getting ahead of himself. Seeing only Floyd humped in sleep in the fire glow and not Willy, Bass turned to the gate and rear wheels of the grub wagon and the vague outline of crates and barrels, the tree cover beyond. Before they could get on the road, before Bass could really get ahead of himself, they would all need to eat.

He recalled the snow-covered valley along Sugar Creek, where Van Dorn's Army of the West had camped for the last time before the Battle of Pea Ridge. For two hours, between hills that slowed the winds, he got to sleep. Only the cooks stayed awake, hustling to make mounds of hardtack for the troops. Then, after two hours, the cooks were sweating and steaming, blowing clouds of ice as they hollered for the slaves to wake up and distribute the hardtack. That was before the army marched in double-quick, as if in a hurry to die.

Bass climbed into the wagon and found what he needed to make hardtack and coffee. He built up the fire and made a level place on rocks to begin cooking. Floyd stirred but didn't fully rouse. Bass was glad to be alone with his thoughts.

People would talk about him how they had talked about him before—believing if Bass and Belle Starr were friends they must be lovers or crooked together in other ways. As if a lawman should only be friends with decent people. As if an outlaw couldn't be decent at times like decent people.

He'd met Belle three years ago at her cabin in Younger's Bend, sixty-two acres her husband, Sam Starr, owned north of a southerly bend of the Canadian River in the Cherokee Nation, about six miles west of Briartown. Bass was rooting for horse thieves he knew were close by but couldn't find, so he thought he'd ask a horse thief what she knew. It was a good excuse to meet her.

The woods were thick around a compound of three single-room cabins linked to each other and situated on a hill about two hundred yards from the river. A brindle German boarhound barked low notes at him from inside a fence of various-sized pickets, which were like the roof boards on each cabin, projecting from the eaves like the fray on a straw hat. The door stood open but empty, then suddenly it wasn't.

"Who the hell is you?" she cawed, then told the dog to hush.

Bass had heard she always wore a black velvet dress to match her black hair, but on that day she wore dingy white brocade and a single-holster gun belt for a Colt .45, like the two he wore.

"I'm not meaning to bother you, ma'am." He tipped his Stetson. "I'm Deputy Marshal Bass Reeves."

She cocked her head doglike to the side. She wasn't wearing a hat, even though he'd heard she always wore one to convince she was a lady. "I figured you was," she said, cawing like his friend James Mershon or anyone else he'd ever met from Kentucky, Tennessee, or West Virginia. She hardly moved as she stood there looking at him. She was petite but statuesque, as if she might be much heavier than her size suggested, and stoic as a dead preacher. "But what makes you feel so welcome on my land? You got a warrant to serve?"

"No, ma'am. I got something else for you, though." He unbuckled a saddle rider and produced a bottle of rye. "We have a lot in common, I hear. Thought we might get acquainted."

Belle smirked. "Well, that's a fine way to go about it." She stepped outside and took a seat in the cane-bottom chair closest to the open door. There were three others in a row beside it. "You can join me a spell. Then you best be on your way."

"Yes, ma'am," he said. He dismounted Strawberry, and Strawberry began those soothing sounds of tearing and chewing grass.

The gate stood open, with grass growing tall around it, as if the gate hadn't been shut in years. The boarhound was big even for a boarhound, the ridge of its back coming to Bass's waist. It continued to remain close by, sniffing and circling him and wagging its tail, as Bass crossed the yard and approached the porch. Belle sat with her legs bent together at the knees as if she were so accustomed to sitting sidesaddle she couldn't sit any other way, while she kept her hands balled side by side in her lap.

Bass decided not to say a word. He sat in the chair next to her, pulled the cork and handed her the bottle. She looked down the neck first, then raised the bottle to her lips. She swallowed twice, then handed the bottle back. He took a drink himself and watched her gaze off in the direction of the river. Maybe at Strawberry going *rip rip chew, rip rip chew*. Or at the boarhound sitting twisted in a knot on the ground and frantically chomping at fleas up and down its tail as if it were an ear of corn.

"A lot in common, huh?" she asked.

Bass handed her the bottle and began telling her about some of his experiences fighting for the Confederacy. He wanted her to know he'd killed hundreds of Yankees, at the Battle of Wilson's Creek, at the Battle of Pea Ridge. "I would've preferred to shoot rebels, mind you," he said, "but to get what you want, sometimes you do what you gotta do."

She remained quiet, pensive, and pulled again at the bottle, so he told her about his first time in Indian Territory. How his master had entered him in a turkey shoot to make money off his sure shot. He laughed, thinking about the Englishman in tails and a top hat who'd matched him all day, shot for shot.

"I was scouting for my brother not too far from Pea Ridge about a month or so before your big battle. It was around Newtonia, across in Missouri, when I was captured. It was February 5 to boot, my sixteenth birthday."

Bass turned to her, but she wasn't looking at him. She still gazed straight ahead, off toward the river. She took another swig and blindly passed him the bottle.

"Bud was my twin brother. He was a captain under Quantrill. Captain Ed Shirley was a helluva bushwhacker. One of the best, you know. He shore hated them Yankees, and boy I still do." She spat a breath, as if the word *Yankees* had left a bad taste, but she didn't otherwise budge.

Bass tipped the bottle up and handed it back to her. "Yours, I'm done," he said, and reached into his coat pocket for his brick of tobacco and bit off a plug. Once he'd nestled into the chair with his legs stretched out, she started up again:

"Bud was on his way home to Carthage, and Major Eno knew it somehow or suspected it. He had me taken to a house he was head-quartered in, the home of a judge. A pretty place, long with red bricks and verandas you could sleep under and a bunch of cherry bushes. You know them by their switches, especially in winter."

She turned to Bass and stared and he studied her staring eyes. They were dark and cold, almost like cherries themselves.

"The major held me there hisself for several hours, so I couldn't warn my brother they had a detachment after him. So he held me there, just me and him in that big old house, but Major Eno was determined to make it small. He fought me and dragged me upstairs to the judge's chamber. You know where I'm going."

Bass nodded.

Belle turned and drummed her nails on the neck of the bottle. "He didn't know I had company outside. A couple of raiders come back for me. I heard a whistle off in the woods I knew wasn't from any of Eno's men." She took a breath that straightened her back and she whistled like a blue jay, even if it was a bit louder than one. "Just like that." She whistled again, and it was just like one that time. "So I knew," she said. "I knew." She chewed her bottom lip. "He had his way with me two times. I took a good beating, but so did he. I was daring him to kill me—the coward." She gripped the bottle's neck with a fist and swirled the rye. "I guess we do have a lot in common.

We got the spring of '62, don't we?" She arched her eyebrows while Bass tugged his mouth to one side. Then she swigged the rye while he spat, and both wiped their mouths on their sleeves.

"He held me a few hours that seemed like forever," she said. "Then that devil major with the meanest blue eyes you ever seen say, 'Well, Myra'—that was my name he put in his mouth and stole from me. I was Myra then, Myra Belle. He say, 'Myra, you can go now. My men will have your brother under arrest before you can reach him.' And with that he flung open the door, so boy I raced outta that room, hurting so as I shot downstairs and run outside, but I had no time to waste cause I knowed I had to stop at them cherry bushes to cut switches.

"'Let her go, let her go,' Major Eno says to his men outside moving like to catch me, not knowing what I knowed—the idiot! So I go, and boy I race away my hurt. I mean, I'm mad as a hornet, not crying any more, just mad and getting madder as I aim to reach the place up the road where they stopped me and jerked me off my mare. And, I swear, I ain't hoping to find my mare waiting there for me, I'm expecting it. And there she was, such a true thing."

Bass loved that part of the story. He lingered in his memory to imagine the moment, but in his way, with Strawberry and not a mare waiting with a sidesaddle to delight sixteen-year-old Belle.

"I raced those thirty-five miles from Newtonia to Carthage like it was nothing," she said. "This was my country. I knew how to ride it and cut it shorter, and I was gonna switch my horse to the grave if I had to. But she didn't make me, the sweet thing. She got me to Carthage before that bastard's detachment. I even had time to change clothes and eat a bite." She stood up and, gazing off toward the river, stomped a bootheel against the porch boards, shocking the boarhound into leaping to its paws and barking. "That's when I heard the cavalry showing up, coming up the road." She turned to Bass and curtseyed. "'Looking for Captain Shirley?' I asked them bastards. 'He ain't here—left half-hour ago. Had business up Spring River. 'Spect he's in Lawrence County by this time.'"

She grinned something crazy-devilish, sending Bass forward in a hurry to spit off the porch before bellowing with laughter he could not control. She watched him with a half-smile, then joined in the laughter, stomping her bootheel several times more.

Bass took out his kerchief and wiped his eyes. "Mercy, that's a good'un."

"But that ain't all," she said, and sat back down as if in a sidesaddle. "That judge's house got a good bushwhacking after I broke them switches—my signal to the raiders in the woods to attack, and they hit it with canons. That sorry bastard Eno would have to mistreat girls somewheres else."

Bass grinned. "You're a hot pistol, Belle Starr."

She smirked. "That's all horseshit, you know. They caught up with Bud a few days later and killed him." She raised the bottle almost to her lips. "I like my little tale lot better," she said, then finished off the rye with two good swallows.

◆ ◆ ◆

Bass was using the points of his badge to poke holes in his hardtack to prevent it from rising when a stirring behind him caught his attention.

He turned and found a whiteness in the shape of a dress hovering over Willy's grave. He squinted to pierce the shadows that the campfire's glow couldn't touch, and he made out lighter-than-white arms and Mary's face. He waved, then looked down and finished making his holes. Her footfalls approached as he was pinning his badge back onto his coat.

"Morning, ma'am," he said, placing the pan of hardtack over the fire.

"Morning," she said, stretching her arms toward the fire to warm her hands as if it were a cold morning.

"How's your husband?" He rubbed his hands together to clean them some, then wiped them on his kerchief.

"Asleep," she said. Her short bangs and shoulder-length hair hung straight and flat as tin so that her face looked like a face inside a bucket.

"Want some coffee?" He reached for the pot to pour another cup for himself, even if she didn't want one.

She lowered her arms and stepped away from the fire in a slow and soundless flotation. Her crinkled eyes welded her caterpillar eyebrows into one, appearing she was about to scold him for something only she and God knew.

"What is it, ma'am?"

"So you killed him?"

Bass studied her. There was a different tone about her now, a different side she was showing. "Bad accident," he said.

"I heard y'all arguing."

Bass turned his attention to the stack of hardtack steaming on Willy's leather apron that Bass had found in the wagon and laid on the ground for such a stacking. He remembered being glad Willy hadn't been wearing it when he died. "Help yourself," he said. He checked on the hardtack that was cooking, then shook his head at Mary, her eyebrows still rigid and dark, like her bucket-like hair. "Doctor couldn't do nothing for him. It's sad. He was a pretty good cook."

"I wouldn't say that, but he was nice to me and my husband." She bent over and tested a hardtack round with a fingertip, and apparently deciding it wasn't too hot, she grabbed one up and then another with her full hands.

"He had demons," said Bass, "but they wasn't all his fault." He sipped his coffee and watched her step closer. He looked at her small pale feet, at her long big toes. He looked up again, and she took a bite of hardtack.

"How about that coffee?" she asked.

"That's right." He turned in circles and found a cup that hardly had anything in it. He slung it empty and wiped the rim against his trousers, then filled it for her.

"Thank you," she said. She was still chewing her first bite. He wondered what she thought about it. He hadn't cooked hardtack in years.

She blew on her coffee and chewed and blew on it again, then gingerly kissed the coffee. She nodded, and he smiled, taking up his turning fork. He turned a hardtack round over in the pan, and it was a nice rye color. So he began turning all of them over.

"They ain't bad," she said.

Bass nodded. He hoped she might grow bored with watching him turn hardtack and wander herself back to her husband. But she stood her ground, twitching her toes. When he finished, he swallowed the last of his coffee and regarded her. She wanted to say something.

"Deputy," she said, tilting her head, "would you let me take my husband home where I can take better care of him?"

He shook his head. "No, ma'am. Can't do that."

"But if you can shoot that cook, surely you can let him go, right?" She hunched her shoulders, and he breathed. He didn't want to do anything else—not speak, not blink. He stared at her without, he hoped, showing one sign of his mounting anger.

"If I let you lay on me while everyone asleep, you could let us go at the next town we come to, right? Say you're giving us to the care of a doctor and you leave and nobody knows nothing. We won't tell. Will you do that? Will you do that for us?" She took a bite of hardtack, and he looked away.

He reached for his kerchief and lifted the pan of hardtack off the fire, then looked at the fire and into it, at the ribbed embers and wisps of smoke, at that watery waving of orange-yellow-red. Mary was behind him still and wasn't moving away. He looked at Floyd in his same sleeping hump, at his hat-darkened face—at his eyes, which shone like stars.

Bass smiled. "Come and get it," he said.

He felt the weight of a spider on his back, the faint pressing of fingertips, as if he might be hot, and he was. "You mean it?" she asked.

◆ ◆ ◆

He shouldn't have been needy. He should've been behind himself, still getting the rest he needed to get one more body closer to filling the Tumbleweed. He shouldn't have been awake this early and leading himself out of the territory from the seat of Willy's grub wagon, with Strawberry tethered in tow. He was ahead of himself in the worst way, to be leading but looking back.

He hesitated to call any part of his feeling a fear. Fear was what he'd felt before he'd ever killed his first white man off a battlefield. Long before he'd gone up from Texas and gone left and stayed in the Seminole Nation until the war was gone, like Willy was gone. He'd killed a man by accident this time. He didn't know if a Black man was allowed to make that mistake. Maybe a deputy could. Maybe a white deputy. Maybe any deputy if the man he'd killed was a Black man like Willy. Even so, before God, he was mad and getting madder at himself for trying so hard to be perfect that he'd forgotten for a time he couldn't be. He was putting distance on himself, true enough. For now, he was still ahead of fear, but he felt far from free.

15

A Hole

On May 6 he registered his prisoners at the jailer's office and delivered Lamar Grayson to the infirmary, with Mary refusing for the third day in a row to regard Bass in any way—always averting her eyes and making that solid caterpillar jut. And when she wasn't clinging to her husband, she held herself in a fast grip, as if she feared what trouble her unruly hands might find. Whenever it was time for her husband's tea, she called for Floyd to boil the water.

Bass had begun to sympathize with her husband, even himself. Perhaps by extension he'd begun to ruminate on a story from the Bible that Pastor Jacob had told on Easter Sunday about the virgin mother putting a pound of ointment to Jesus's feet, how dry they must have been, and how his mother then wiped his feet with her hair. They were in the company of Lazarus, sitting there at the dinner table like a newborn baby, and Judas, like the devil himself. Bass had thought on that scene a lot as they had ridden the ruts and coughed hot dust the previous day.

Why, he wondered, would Jesus allow a scoundrel like Judas to join his outfit? That one was easy for Bass to answer. Sometimes a body just feels bad for a sorry soul. But how could any two feet need or even take that much ointment? And how dry as kindling must Mary's hair have been to be of any use? That seemed to him a miracle, a miracle within a miracle. He could come up with nothing to explain it all. It was a small bodily mystery, but it was a big one too.

Last night, before allowing the prisoners to eat, he had preached on that story. About Jesus's dry feet and his mother's virgin-smelling hair, and about the need to care for others like Lazarus and Judas, who were different as night and day and left and right, and about the little mysteries we always needed to pay attention to and be thankful for. Men were too busy chasing big things, big money and big fights and big drunken cabbage feasts. What we needed was to remember our mamas, who raised us to be good as they were.

Mary and the men had remained quiet and nonresponsive throughout his sermon and after it. Bass alone had said Amen before he and Floyd passed out hardtack rounds and cups and gourds of water.

◆ ◆ ◆

He needed his family like his family needed him. He needed to do anything but wait, but he waited for the clerk to fill out his bank check and get it signed and cashed out. He paid Floyd what he owed him for the trip, and outside the courthouse he found James Mershon in a knot of other deputies shooting the bull.

They stood behind the courthouse in the angular shade of the gallows. It was no hanging day, so it was quiet this midafternoon except for the men's laughter and the buzz of insects and the groans of hot prisoners suffocating in the stench of the basement jail.

James was telling about the time an armadillo had crawled inside his house and ate half of a pecan pie, so Bass was slow to walk up, letting him finish.

"So," James said, "what do you boys think the first thing I did about that armadillo was after I sat down and ate the other half of my pecan pie?"

The deputies—Bud Ledbetter, Wood Bailey, Jacob Yoes—folded over with laughter.

James remained erect even as he chuckled with them, patting their backs and looking from one to the other. When he noticed Bass, his face fell and paled. He broke from the ring.

"Bass, I've got a bone to pick with you." He pulled Bass aside and turned his back to the others. "Family of Bywaters comes to my home the other night. They barge right in and in front of my wife and children start demanding to know why I shot a law-abiding shopkeeper. You was playing with that news report but they wasn't. They accused me of murder, saying if I don't prove he was a whiskey peddler with that Webb fella and I don't hang up there on that roost, they'll shoot me and my whole family dead. Now, I whipped their asses good to get out, but still, Bass, in front of my young'uns?"

Bass's eyes trailed to the gallows. A warm wind nudged the four nooses hanging in wait for the next execution. It was a perfect silence for him to think about every mistake he'd made.

"Nah!" James said, slapping Bass's back. "Just messing with you, Bass."

"You had me," Bass said, trying to smile.

"Yeah, I did. You should've seen your face."

Bass let his half-smile fade and pulled James aside another step, even though the other deputies were already walking back toward the courthouse. "I need to tell you something."

James took off his hat, and sweat ran down around his eyes. "Yeah?" He drew a kerchief from his pocket and mopped his face and sopping thin hair, then put his hat back down on his head.

"Had a incident in I.T."

They studied each other's eyes. James always had pretty blue ones.

"You ain't trying to get me?" James asked.

Bass shook his head. "Willy Leach, my cook, he passed. Had a bad accident in camp three nights ago in the Chickasaw Nation near Cherokee Town."

"What happened?"

"Don't rightly know," Bass said. "Was emptying my Winchester to clean it. We was sitting around talking, about to eat. A stray bull pup created a ruckus begging for a bite, and then I fired, know that." He wondered how to keep wording it, so it would sound like the truth and be the truth both. He didn't believe he should hang. "Didn't mean to like that, James. I wasn't aiming to kill Willy, but the bullet nicked him deep in the neck. I fetched a doctor, but he already had done give up the ghost."

"Nat Hawkins?" James asked.

Bass nodded.

"Anybody else there with you?"

"Floyd Wilson."

James nodded. "Hate to hear it, Bass. Hard to lose good help. The territory's a tough place for good help. You can't have my cook, dammit, but I'll ask around if anybody knows of anybody."

Bass nodded and held out his hand. "Thank you, James. And you don't mind writing up a report for me?"

"Sure, sure," James said. He leaned in, still shaking Bass's hand. "I had you, didn't I?"

Bass grinned. "You had me."

James released his grip and set his hands on his hips and shook his head. "Only because you ain't yourself, off thinking about other things. You need to go home to your family and get some rest."

"Need to," Bass said.

"Don't think about going out again any time soon, hear? You just got Webb. That's a get of a lifetime."

Bass nodded.

"I wanna hear you tell it sometime, but you go on get your rest now, hear?"

"Aiming to," Bass said. He tried to smile, then turned and waved and walked for Strawberry, tied on the north side of the courthouse. He listened to James's boots following, sweeping the ground behind him with a steady pace, as if he was working a field with a scythe back toward the courthouse or the jail cells below it.

◆ ◆ ◆

Bass stopped at the commissary within the fort and found himself nearly out of breath as he milled the two sacks of hominy, the flotsam of corn dust swirling in the air about him. Then, with his mother's grits laid across his lap, he trotted Strawberry homeward.

He thought of a time when he didn't have a horse at all to trust. A year ago, when he walked for two full days. The newspapers liked blood so they wrote longer about it. Everyone in and around the law liked it better than he did because he didn't like it at all. James might think Webb was Bass's biggest get, and he was big, but Bass knew the Coldirons were his biggest, being bloodless, and he wouldn't easily change his mind.

He hadn't the energy to stay angry at himself for letting Willy push him off his perfect space. For trying to change him with his darker darkness. Bass was dust-covered from a sorrel-colored dust. He was sweaty, too, from death after death, and he was tired, tired. He and Strawberry both were.

He'd known all along he'd need to be different.

When they reached the Arkansas River, Johnny Russom's ferry was banked on the other side and picking up passengers. It was picking up the night, too, dragging it behind but coming still, peeking with a closed eye behind the Van Buren bluff.

Something about the wait by the water and his unknowable future, like the night coming on, reminded him of Yah-kee, the Cherokee medicine man who'd come close to killing him two years earlier. The Jewish chief priests had wanted Lazarus dead again and to stay that way.

Bass had telegraphed the court from the Creek Nation requesting the marshal to send him a writ for Tee-see-yah-kee Tadpole, better known as Yah-kee, though he sometimes went by John. Bass had rounded up a gang of horse thieves in North Fork Town that filled two wagons. Two of the prisoners had complained to him that they had each given Yah-kee a pony for a conjurbag that the old man had guaranteed would make them invisible should any officers attempt to arrest them. Bass had laughed upon hearing that, understanding only then why the two white boys had stood their ground and grinned when he'd put his pistols on them.

When Bass had received his writ, he left Floyd and Willy to guard the prisoners while he paid Yah-kee an early morning visit. He dismounted at the stable, and sure enough he found the stolen ponies the prisoners had described, both with a recent brand not completely covering an old one. Yah-kee must have heard him ride up and seen him head into the stable because he was standing on his porch with the front door closed behind him, appearing ready to go with him.

Yah-kee was dressed in a faded-red turban and bowtie, though instead of wearing it in a bow, as Bass did, the old man had tied his in a knot, cowboy style. His trousers were missing buttons, so his white shirt showed through. In a large, swollen hand he carried a walking stick with a gourd rattle fixed on top to show he was the village medicine man, and in another he held a sack of crabapples.

On the way back to camp, with Yah-kee riding one of the ponies, Bass began to feel stiff and sore in his back. The next day, on the return to Fort Smith, the soreness had spread to his limbs. His eyes became so swollen by noon he could scarcely see. He didn't want anything to eat, but he seemed possessed of a consuming thirst. When they reached a good spot on Alabama Creek, he decided the outfit needed to stop and make camp so that he could drink as much as he wanted and take a nap. When he woke hours later, he had no ability to stand. He'd heard old timers describe gout, and he wondered if that was what was afflicting him all over, if that was what the old medicine man suffered in his hands. If Yah-kee had somehow passed it on to him.

He couldn't see well because of his blurred vision and because now it was night. A moonless night. The prisoners looked to be shackled together in a row along the bank, like shrubs of snakeweed. Some of the men snored to the chirping and barking of frogs. Bass was convinced that Yah-kee had put a spell on him, that such a thing was possible in a Christian world, if the devil was going to live in it too.

He crawled on his hands and knees until he believed he'd found the old man. He strained to see as if in a deep hole, and the medicine man appeared in parts—his turban, his walking stick in the crook of an arm, his sleeping eyes, his frowning mustache and broomy goatee that gave him, he realized only then, a striking resemblance to Bass's old master, George Reeves. Had God abandoned him to allow the past to ride up on him in a fury, hauling all his sins and all his blessings back upon him for a debt he now owed?

Bass strained to lift an arm to reach out and shake him and he saw a white tail-like thing hanging out of Yah-kee's coat pocket. He could only think that there must have been a mouse, an albino mouse, in his pocket, a little thing the old man cherished and fed crabapples. But it didn't move when Bass touched it, so he stilled his shaking hand long enough to pinch the tail or tail-like thing between his fingers and tug on it, and there was something like a mouse at the other end of it, but it was dark and still, maybe dead.

Not until he held the smooth thing in his hand did he understand what it probably was, so he dragged himself away, closer to the fire, to look at it. Sweating and wheezing, nearly out of breath, he blinked and strained. It was indeed a mole-skin bag, cinched by a string. He worked the opening loose and turned the bag upside down, and out upon the ground fell a grassy wad of tobacco, he first suspected, but there was hair in the wad, too, and roots and pebbles—and all of that was bound by tiny red and yellow string.

He shut his eyes and said a prayer, asking the Lord to forgive him for his pride, if that was what had allowed that old man to put a death spell on him. He recited the Twenty-Third Psalm, then put the conjuring thing back into the bag, cinched it tight, and flung it with a grunt with all his might over the row of prisoners. He listened for the little splash of water but could only imagine it floating away on the bosom of the creek.

He already ached less and breathed better. Maybe that was the Lord lightening his load.

"Bazz, what have you done?" It was Yah-kee. His words were of sorrow from the dark, from the snakeweed and creek water. "You stole my conjurbag."

"I did," Bass said, his tongue sticking to the roof of his mouth.

There was a moment of nothing but frogs as Bass pressed his hands against the ground in an attempt to rise to his feet.

"You would've been dead before we reached Fort Smith."

Bass wagged his head. "I expect sooner."

◆ ◆ ◆

Bass only pretended to listen to Johnny's high accounts. He heard him squawk laughter. Then Bass said goodnight and walked Strawberry off Johnny's ferry to climb the bluff.

A get of a lifetime, Bass thought, passing along Second Street as erect in the saddle as he could sit and greeting his white neighbors along the way. He'd arrested more than his fair share of outlaws. He'd killed more than his fair share, too. And with that fair and unfair share of bounties came his showplace. Not even night coming on could dim its glory.

With money he'd saved from his first paid work after emancipation as a cowboy for Caesar Bruner and then a scout for bounty hunters, he'd bought five acres of land in downtown Van Buren, at the corner of Second and Vine. For two hundred dollars in 1873. For nearly a year, he'd devoted himself to the construction of the eight-room farmhouse. For the foundation, he hauled twelve cypress stumps behind horses out of the bogs along the Arkansas River. He felled and planed oak, ash, and cedar to construct the floor, walls, roof, and shingles. From two wagonloads of limestone from the quarry northward on Beaver Lake, he built two double-sided fireplaces and, with Jennie's help, painted the house buttercup yellow, including the porch rails and steps, even the picket fence that faced the street. His final touch, he transplanted saplings from the river banks—redbuds, dogwoods, and mimosas. Five and a half miles southeast of the old Reeves plantation, his showplace stood as a monument to everything he believed was good and right and fair and unfair and true and untrue about Negroes.

Silhouettes flitted past windows, while outside there was no one, his eyes sweeping over only the unfilled spaces between the houses—until one did appear, dropping like an apple out of the mimosa closest to the front porch and then running toward him on the lane on churning legs, running hard on bare feet. It was ten-year-old Bennie, his bare chest hardly visible against the backdrop of the dirt lane.

Bass pulled up and watched Bennie stop and grin and heave air.

"Son," he said, "that was quite a gallop."

Bennie continued to grin. "Watch this," he said, and he ran back to the mimosa and climbed up and vanished among the leaves and limbs.

Bass waited for him to drop again, fast and with a thump, but his son remained hidden, quiet. In case Bennie was watching, Bass waved at him before turning Strawberry off the lane to unload the grits.

He rode up to his mother's and auntie's porch, and the door flew open.

"Son!" Pearlalee said, already dressed in her nightgown with her hair combed out.

Auntie Totty appeared behind her, wide-eyed over Pearlalee's shoulder. A yellowed kerchief was tied about her head. "Bass?"

Bass smiled and patted what was across his lap. "Look what I found." He tossed a sack of grits to the ground and then the other one on top of it, and a small cloud-like breath puffed out from a hole he hadn't realized was there.

Pearlalee stepped outside. "Goodness, grits I see?"

"Yes, ma'am."

Pearlalee laughed and clasped her hands. "Hallelujah!"

Auntie Totty stepped outside to see and stood just as white in her nightgown next to her sister. She gazed silently at Bass. "You back early, Bass."

"Yeah," Bass said, "you right. Quick this time." He wasn't sure he wanted to get into it yet.

Pearlalee let her hands fall by her hips. "Something wrong, son?"

"You get your money?" Auntie Totty asked.

Bass nodded. "Some of it." He dismounted and Strawberry bent to nibble the sprigs of grass growing in islands in the vast dirt yard. "Got who I went after most," he said, clutching a sack in each hand and stepping up to the porch, "then had to come back." He set the sacks down on either side of him and grasped a porch post to lean on. He looked through the open door, at the empty spaces in their two-room house, and rubbed his fingers over the grooves of the wood. He looked at Pearlalee, at Auntie Totty, who was much thinner and beginning to appear frail.

"What is it, son?" Pearlalee asked. "You kill someone?"

Inside the house his eyes settled on what was there—his mother's butter urn, standing but also leaning, like he was, beside Auntie Totty's lamp-lit loom, hunched over as if on all fours like something starved, its warp strings glowing white like ribs. He often thought of his grandmammy stooped at the stove with a hand braced on her knee, and of Sugar, his grandfather, rocking and chewing, whenever he peered in, wanting to see them, almost expecting to. "More than one," he said.

"Lord forgives you," Pearlalee said. She walked to the edge of the porch and reached out and touched his arm, but he pulled his arm away.

"I'll soil you," he said.

Pearlalee scratched the dry skin on her elbows and gave him a pained smile. "Lord loves you."

Bass nodded. "I'm blessed then."

"Glory be," Auntie Totty said.

Bass nodded and let his eyes settle on his dusty boots. He let himself keep nodding and took a breath. "I killed one a us this time."

"Can't let your guard down around your own people," Pearlalee told him. "We ask to die too, don't we?"

"Sometimes."

"Did this one?" Auntie Totty asked.

Bass kicked the ground with his heel, then eased his boot down flat. He looked up, and both were squinting at him as if he weren't there yet before them. He loved them and knew they loved him. He wasn't so far away. "He asked for it, I thought," he said. He filled his lungs and crossed his arms. They still squinted, and he remembered the broad outline of his father, his whipped back to him, from so long ago, who was never going to show again. His mother's hair looked dry and colorless.

"A lot do," he said to break the silence. "Easy sometimes to just give them what you think they're asking you for, but maybe he wasn't asking for what I thought. Maybe he was a bluff, just a bad wind blowing, and I needed to just let it pass. Just let him be."

"Sound like something couldn't be helped," Pearlalee said.

Bass reached down for both sacks. "Accidents ain't always accidents, though," he said and started taking the steps. "I mean, it ain't a accident if I meant to shoot him."

Pearlalee shuffled in front of him and placed her palms on his chest. "Did you mean to kill him? Say it. Just me and Totty here. Just us and the Good Lord."

Bass licked his mustache off his lips and realized how thirsty he was. "I don't think so, Mama. Really don't. I don't think I even meant to shoot him." He spoke without looking at her. Without knowing what he was looking at. "I meant to shoot Master Reeves. To kill him, maybe so."

16

The Blackness

For three days, beginning on Friday, he prayed in every way he knew and in every way he learned but always with an ear out for the road. He sometimes uttered, sometimes muttered, and sometimes sang with Jennie for the truth, so he would know it, and for the words, so he could say it, and for God's mercy, if Willy, if serving the table of God, agreed Bass deserved it.

He hadn't deliberately killed Willy. But he could be charged with manslaughter or negligent homicide, unless he had a case he'd acted in self-defense, if a good pup and a good sorrel could be deemed parts of the self. Surely, Willy had softened by now and grown to love all things and would pipe up to keep Bass out of the federal jail if he had anything to add.

He took a long bath in Jennie's too-small tub the first night home and talked to her of all things on his mind, while she sat in a pulled-up chair with her feet in his hands in the water.

"Are you thinking it'll be like last time?" she asked.

His eyes trailed up her dark legs, into her white nightgown. He rubbed her feet and pondered what she meant. His past was littered with last times. "Last time?" He looked up to her face.

"When they charged you for attempting to murder that man in Eureka Springs."

Jennie was really taking him to the beginning. He'd been a deputy for a matter of only a few months when in late summer of 1875 he found himself in a fight for his life. The hotel up on a mountainside that overlooked Basin Spring had called for a deputy to arrest a young Osage man for shutting himself into a room and refusing to leave after other tenants had complained that he had beaten up his female companion and then threatened to do the same to the owner if he didn't stay out of his private business and leave him be. Bass had knocked on the door to his hotel room, and the Osage had told him to stay clear of the door or he'd shoot him through it, so Bass proposed that they meet outside at the spring, which was known to have healing properties. And that's where Bass went. He took the many stairs down the mountainside to the park with the spring, which was ice cold and felt good splashed on his face and open eyes, and Bass drank as much as he could drink. When he was drying his face on his kerchief, he felt a tug at his waist and then saw the young round-faced Osage with no eyebrows with one of his Colt .45s in his hands.

The two wrestled with the pistol and then punched and kneed each other in a twisted fury as they rolled on the ground, until Bass found the upper hand and beat him close to death, breaking the Osage's nose and jaws and knocking out eight of his teeth. The trouble came when the court discovered that the Osage was not an Osage. He was actually a Missouri-born hillbilly who liked to pretend to be Indian, which called into question Bass's legal authority to arrest him. The jury found him not guilty, but the court's decision to bring charges in the first place had taught Bass an important lesson about moderation, even in defense of his life.

"Different cases, don't you think?"

Jennie shrugged one shoulder. She kept her arms crossed, her hands tucked. "I hope. Now, don't take this the wrong way," she said, "I'm just asking to ask. But would you have beaten that man as badly if you had known he was white?"

Bass stopped rubbing her hard feet.

"What would it matter?" But that wasn't what he'd meant to say. "I've beaten up plenty white people. And killed plenty. You know that."

"Did you have to when you did?"

"Yes, I believe I did."

"Did you have to go as far with that man you thought was an Osage? Could you have let up some? Could you have let up on Willy some? Would you have shot him if he was white? I'm asking is all."

Bass felt a rage rising in him, while she looked so loose. She was almost smiling at him, was too beautiful for the moment for it to make sense.

"I don't know, I think so."

"Who taught you to treat white people special? Whose fault is that, Bass?"

"Jennie, that ain't it. Maybe I just expect more outta us. We weren't born from evil. We was robbed before our first breath, so we can unlearn the evil shit we been taught."

"Unlearn everything? Really, Bass? Can't only God on high learn and unlearn everything?" She uncrossed her arms and pulled her feet out of the water. She leaned forward to hold his head, and it felt good to him to be held that way, for her to be this close, seeing everything there was to see in him. "Bass, baby, you need to let up on yourself too." She kissed him and then hugged him as if he were her little boy.

◆ ◆ ◆

The next morning Bass sat with the young'uns beside him and on his lap and apologized he'd returned from being gone with nothing but grits at grandmammy's and an outlaw's revolver and scabbard. He explained the relevance of the eleven notches and how Webb had told him before dying, "I expected you to make twelve," which wowed the kids for a moment. Bennie wanted to take the pistol outside to shoot it. Then Lula asked her father if he really didn't bring back any candy. Bass tried to explain chaos in a way they could understand by describing a hailstorm. Then he tried to explain to Robert what had happened to Fringe at Bywaters's Store, such a good bay gelding, but words for such things never satisfied. You couldn't go pluck the right ones off a tree.

He walked over to Sallie's and spoke to her and her husband and held his granddaughter against his shoulder and cheek and ear and nose, wanting to smell that smell and hear and feel that purring weight forever. Then he led the cloud of young'uns to the other house next door and ate a bowl of grits and a salted onion out on the porch with Pearlalee and Auntie Totty. He'd slept fine, he said. Then he checked on Strawberry, and Strawberry checked on him.

Strawberry's weary black eyes told Bass they both needed more rest, so Bass waited until the next day, on Saturday, to tack him for a ride across town to visit Pastor Jacob.

Bass spotted him from around the corner before he could even see the whitewashed church building good. He could see him equal to the trees but bowed over at the peak of the tin roof. Could hear the hammering coming from somewhere long before that.

"Pastor," Bass called.

Pastor Jacob straightened and waved the hand with the hammer and made to move.

"No, I'll come up to you." Bass liked to climb a ladder and stand on a roof.

He tied Strawberry to a post and looked up at Pastor Jacob, wiping his face on his sleeve. The happy chirp of a butcher bird sounded from a nearby tree. Bass watched for a lone swath of gray and its black mask as he approached the ladder, and as he climbed. He hadn't seen or heard a butcher bird in some years.

Pastor Jacob met him with a handshake. "Bass, God bless you, so good to see you."

"Same, Pastor J," Bass said. He saw the roll of tar paper wedged against a sheet of tin that had been pulled up from its nails and folded back. "Anything I can help you with?"

"Got a leak taking care of."

"That same one or new one?"

Pastor Jacob laughed. "Both."

Bass smiled and squinted from the glare of the sun on tin.

Pastor Jacob retreated crookedly across the pitch of the roof with his arms out for balance. Bass leaned as he followed but hung his arms down at their sides. He watched Pastor Jacob ease to his haunches at the tar paper.

Pastor Jacob rolled out a sheet and picked up a knife to cut it. "What about you?" he asked. "Anything I can help you with?"

"Well," Bass said, "thinking about how many faces Satan has."

Pastor Jacob laughed. "You know there as many as there are people."

Bass smirked, then noticed his shadow split the pastor's face, half in sun, half in shade, so he shifted his stance to place it over him, and the pastor's eyes relaxed, deepened.

"Come to pray?"

Bass nodded. "Can't quite feed my soul."

"Course, anytime, Bass, you know that. Any time, any place." He set his knife down. "I start and you finish?"

Bass lowered to his bootheels. "Sound good." He shut his eyes and touched the hot tin with his fingertips. The butcher bird was singing now from a closer tree. This time it had no quit, trilling and then whistling cleanly like Bass might, with two whole notes on an upward stairstep before dropping an octave for another upward two-note stairstep. It was speaking to Bass like Pastor Jacob was speaking, like together they were voicing something for Bass he couldn't quite understand. He had a mind like Lazarus to peek, and a mind like Judas to run.

◆ ◆ ◆

That evening, after supper, Jennie took Bass's hand and led him from the dining room to the parlor and sat him down on the settee.

"Something for your spirit," she said. She patted his hands stacked on his crossed knees and retreated in her black bustle dress to the dining room, where the young'uns giggled and couldn't stay hid, sometimes peeking and ducking back.

Bass would smile to show he saw them. He'd point and make faces. But he would also listen beyond the room to the sky because the sky didn't only twinkle. It could cloud up to announce the coming and going of cattle, meaning it could announce in a different place something else.

All nine of the children who still lived at home assembled before him to present a play of the song "The Farmer in the Dell." Because the little ones could never keep a secret, he thought he knew what to expect, but when they entered one by one donning articles they'd plundered from his trunk of territory clothes, his hands left his lap for the settee's red velvet upholstery, as if in search of what he felt about that.

He grinned nevertheless. He grinned for some time, for the little ones especially, like his granddaddy Sugar had grinned—as much in anticipation of the master's presence as in his presence. Bass grinned like he'd seen men grin in death once rigor mortis had set in. As if a grin was a mustache you could remove and hang back on your face upside down.

Jennie followed the last of the children and took a seat at the piano, her bustle and crinoline skirt hiding her feet at the pedals. Before he left for Indian Territory, the children usually sang and danced, until the whole house shimmied. A farewell performance was Jennie's way of reminding Bass how much they'd miss him for the two or three or four weeks he'd be gone. This was the first time they'd performed upon his return.

The oldest, eighteen-year-old Robert in patched overalls and a cowboy kerchief, played the farmer who took a wife, played by the next oldest, sixteen-year-old Harriet wearing the bonnet that one of Miss Laura's prostitutes had thrown in Bass's face in a fit outside the courthouse in Fort Smith for arresting her son. Robert and Harriet, both beautifully dark like their mother, had become indispensable to Jennie with the chores. Then, as the song went, Robert and Harriet took ten-year-old Bennie as their child. He was the most childish of the lot, whose head was entirely swallowed up by the floppy felt hat shot with bullet holes.

On cue, Bennie pushed the hat theatrically out of his eyes, at a high tilt far back on his head, allowing Bass to recognize all over again how his son's oval, delicate face, with the short eyebrows high over wide-set eyes, the full but small mouth, the small, rounded ears, like trigger guards, the skin no darker than cypress, the freckles across the nose and upper cheeks, made a perfect cameo—a mirror image of Bass as a young Bass.

Bass continued to use muscles in his face that he rarely used away from home, until Bennie forgot to say what he in turn would take. Jennie whispered the answer and so did Harriet, but Bennie remained frozen, staring at Bass as though he didn't recognize him as his father and was too shy to speak.

Bass leaned forward and hunched low, his elbows on his knees. "Go ahead, son," he said. "You got it. You know it."

But Bennie wouldn't budge. He'd always been stubborn, mischievous, and hot-tempered. At least that had been his way as a baby and toddler—a real happy-go-lucky little thing until he didn't get what he wanted, and then Katy bar the door, he'd screech and buck, throwing his head back or charging on all fours until he rammed something.

Bass grew quiet amid Jennie's continuous piano-playing.

Fourteen-year-old Georgia, dressed in a lavender garden hat and a white nurse's apron, finally prodded Bennie in the gut, and Bennie mooed.

"Not a *cow*!" Georgia stomped, though invisibly underneath the dragging hem of the apron, while the hat, mounded with satin roses and a white peony, teetered wildly on her head, threatening to fall. Bass had worn the hat once to hide his face at a funeral to apprehend Dick Glass, as he'd only worn the apron once, when assisting a doctor two years back on the autopsy of poor Lydia Combs of the Choctaw Nation. He remembered her lungs, virtually dry, not bloated, not clotted, but looking so much like bass meat, even though her old body had been found on a sand bar in Lee's Creek.

"You're a child, a *child*, Bennie!" Georgia yelled.

Bennie flashed a grin at Bass.

Not knowing what else to do, he didn't know the boy, Bass grinned back.

"*The child takes a nurse*," Georgia said. "Say it! You know it!"

"Come on, Bennie," the others chimed.

Jennie played on, looping the melody as if it were a lasso, as if she were in her own calm cowboy world, and Bass envied her.

Bennie kept grinning, trying to coax Bass to keep grinning too, but Bass let his own grin disappear behind the curtains of his mustache. To be stern, he hiked his eyebrows and sat up straight.

Bennie turned to Georgia, giving her a real sourpuss face. "The *cow* takes a nurse," he belted, not on the beat at all, and shot a grin back at Bass.

Bass half-smiled but doubted it was even the half-right thing to do. Then, as if to save him, the family chorus rushed in, singing, *"Heigh-ho, the derry-o, the child takes a nurse."*

The rest of the song went on without a hitch. The nurse, played by Georgia—who'd loved cows ever since Bass had given her a *Harper's New Monthly* picture of a white milkmaid surrounded by horned cows, which she'd tacked on the wall above her side of the bed—naturally took a cow, a part she also played, swaying on her heels and pretending to chew.

Then Georgia as the cow took a pig, Newland, easily the messiest eater and dresser of the bunch. He wore the beaded buckskin jacket Caesar Bruner had given Bass in 1862, which had been the first thing Bass ever wore that a white man had never touched. Bass grinned at the rolled-up sleeves.

Then Newland took a dog. Because Edgar, leaning on a cane, loved dogs.

Alice, holding a raccoon cap behind her back and flipping the tail from side to side, was the cat. Bass could only guess why.

With moccasins on her hands and a woolen sash as a tail, Lula was the mouse, a perfect little mouse.

And two-year-old Homer, appearing armless underneath a poncho, was the cheese. Because cheese was heavy and silent and soft and peaceful. Homer had learned a few words but rarely spoke them. He preferred to watch, to listen, and to dance. He'd been the first of the ten children to be born while Bass was home, and with the midwife down at the time with the crud, Bass had caught Homer himself. Sticky and white, Homer could have been cheese then, too.

He'd never felt more dishonest, when all he'd ever wanted was to be honest. He'd been away from home in a gamble to make his home a godly home and to make the world around it godly, but he'd been away, losing himself among the godless, for stretches too long. These people weren't his, or his completely, only vaguely, a reminiscence. It was as if he'd died years ago and was remembering to look on from where he was, so where was he?

◆ ◆ ◆

He woke before sunup on the third day, on Sunday, May 9, craving coffee, craving heat, and thinking about everyone and everything he risked losing. After the war he'd found Pearlalee and Auntie Totty where the old master, the father, had freed them, living not far from where they lived now, on the old plantation, in Sugar's cabin, and slaving for food and a roof the same way they always had. Bass thanked the Lord, though, that he'd found them easily and alive and not dead and buried, like Sugar who'd vanished without a physical trace that he'd ever lived. Not even his cane stood in a corner, and there were no clothes in a box. There was nothing but memory and a place outside in the dark by the same old mimosa to point to. To avoid seeing Master Reeves, Bass had tied his pony in the woods and walked on at night.

Jennie had been harder to track. Rub alone still lived on the old plantation in Texas, residing in Mr. Hagan's cabin, since Mr. Hagan had gone west to seek whatever the white world offered ex-overseers. Rub was Rub, always one irritable groom, so he didn't care to speak, giving only a vague notion of where Bass could find her. "Running off behind Winnie for a city life" was all Rub knew to say, or would say.

Bass had prayed urgently then as he prayed now, that the Good Lord would guide him straight. He passed throngs of freed Negroes, mostly on foot, hanging the mourning face of soldiers as they lined the roads and congregated for scraps behind every business and home, fishing and gigging along every mud bank, who all prayed, too. When he didn't find the cousins in nearby Pottsboro, he prayed for fewer bends, the fewest, and was longer at praying, harder with it, as he rode to Sherman. When he didn't find them there, he prayed for no more bends at all—*please, dear God*—approaching tears, and then, in Paris, he found Jennie and Winnie working at an inn and sleeping in the stable behind it.

Winnie had found lovers at the inn, an endless stream of them, white and Negro and Indian and some so mixed they were just people, just men whom she never wished to leave, saying, "Go if you got. Go, go, but I'm here and staying."

The Seminoles he'd lived among for the last two years of the war wouldn't let him leave them with nothing and had given him the pony. Within a few months of finding Jennie and walking her on the pony back to Arkansas, he would trade that pony for a horse more appropriate for his size. He'd eventually trade that horse for the sorrel he'd name Strawberry. He thanked the Lord for one and the next—for all the chains that bound him in this moment of his life to so much else. He shouldn't have shot Willy in a neck he hardly had. The hominy was what Willy had wanted. Bass should've thought to give him some. He shouldn't have let him leave without first trying that.

◆ ◆ ◆

When the Frisco whistled on the outskirts of town that cloudless afternoon, after church service and dinner, Bass quickly became encircled by young'uns begging to see the passenger train from Memphis and Saint Louis and Fayetteville chug into the station across the street. Greeting the train had become a Van Buren tradition, and a Reeves one.

"Let's get to it!" he said, and they all scrambled outside, with Jennie and Harriet appearing to dance down the steps of the porch with their skirt hems held high. Already the engine's steaming black chimney stood with immensity as if a permanent fixture on the horizon. It was how Bass imagined a whale to rise and spray and loom before its slow collapse. It was how Bass imagined a whale to be—that black, since most as they tell it were. A host of coal-faced white men always hung dog-tired but proud from both sides as if by feeding it and keeping the clockwork motion of rods and wheels moving moving moving they'd moved it even without its help. He never much considered the ghostly sleepy passengers, dressed as if for a funeral. The youngest of his young'uns would wave and wave at them until some of them behind the windows waved back. They would become obsessed with waving, were already waving and squealing now, as if they couldn't help it.

A pilgrimage of townsfolk in their best jackets and trousers and hats and dresses emerged up and down Second Street, scissoring and jouncing into the white heat, against a low white sky. Past the braking train, at the end of the street, blurred by heat as if under clear but waving water, horses clopped.

Bass watched his young'uns scatter toward the weeds along the raised tracks, their squeals absorbed by the squealing wheels and spits of steam, and in the gust of heat, his young'uns persisted with their persistent waving.

Jennie took Bass's arm and leaned into him. "Don't matter the reason, I'm glad you're home, Bass."

He kissed her uncovered head. Her hair, drawn back, was ribbed but smooth as a feather. "We been through many a tight spot together, ain't we?" He smirked and turned to the three chestnut quarter horses no one else appeared to notice.

When deputy marshals James Mershon and Sonny Fair reached the showplace lane and picket fence, with a riderless horse in tow, Bass whistled.

James looked first, then both turned their horses his way.

Bass took Jennie's hand and squeezed it. "They're here."

"Who?" she asked, surveying the townspeople among them.

He turned her to the horses walking up behind them. She knew James, and Sonny's badge twinkling from the sun like a real star told her who he was.

Bass paused to look her in her terrified eyes. "Get with Theodore Barnes. Him first." He nodded. "I'll be all right. Have him see me Monday morning as early as can be." She looked like she didn't understand, but he knew that was her way of storing every word. "I love you, Jennie Jennie," he said. That was something he hadn't said to her in years. She was twice what other women were so he should call her name twice, and that's what he'd done for a few days, maybe a week, until she told him sternly he could quit. The memory sparked a smile from her, and that was enough, all he needed, before he stepped away, tipping his hat.

"James, Sonny," he said, feeling the jagged edge of where Webb's bullet had cut the brim. He laughed and removed his hat as he stood on James's side because he knew James better and liked him. He knew Sonny to be an old Confederate, like Marshal Carroll, and didn't like him. "I need me a new one, don't I? Jim Webb went and left his mark on me, but I hate to lose a thing that fits so right, you know?" He grinned against their implacable faces and set his hat back on his head.

"We've come to arrest you," Sonny said. His voice was a series of sharp grunts, as if he'd never learned to fully open this throat to speak. Even his clothes appeared tight and strangling.

Bass consulted James, who was gazing away at the train as if transfixed by it and flexing a hand around his saddle horn. Bass looked back at Sonny, who seemed too small to be here, to be doing this. "What for?"

"What do you think?" Sonny pulled a hand out of a pocket and held up a warrant, creased from being folded. "For the murder of William Leach, what for."

"Murder?" Bass said. "For a accident?"

James pivoted birdlike to Bass. "We talked to Floyd. He said you was cleaning your rifle. A cartridge jammed, he thought. But your prisoners tell a different story, and one ain't even a prisoner. They tell of a dispute you and Floyd never told of. Something about a dog."

"I told you about a dog," Bass said.

"But you didn't tell about a dispute," James said.

Bass grinned and shook his head. "With Willy, there was always a dispute. That don't mean nothing."

"You killed your n—— because he's a n——, didn't you?" Sonny asked. "Not that I blame you, but it's a new day. The one you wanted, right? Law's the law now, boy."

Bass turned to James. "Murder? Not manslaughter? Not negligence, huh? Straight to murder, for a neck wound?"

"That's how Commissioner Wheeler and Marshal Carroll and me see it," Sonny said.

"I'm along to be along because we're close, you and me," James said, "but we're taking you in, Bass. We're arresting you today."

Coal smoke from the train drifted past, veiling him and them. He turned to find Jennie in the belly of smoke and chatter. She was rounding up the young'uns with harsh orders. Georgia, Harriet, and Robert stood gravely looking on while Bennie and the rest kept their faces angled up at the windows. Refusing to hear their mother and be corralled, they continued to jump and wave as if the train might suddenly lift off its rails and flee into the depths of unknowable space.

2. The federal "Hell on the Border" jail at Fort Smith National Historic Site, in Fort Smith, Arkansas. © Jim West / agefotostock.

17

A Case

Bass sat on his coat in a darkened corner, with his back against the mortared limestone, and wiped his mustache from the corners of his mouth—first the left side, then the right, then the left side again and the right side again—as he watched the morning light, nearly with trepidation, trespass the grated windows on both ends of the fifty-five-foot-long jail cell. It illuminated little more than the windows themselves and the ceiling planks directly above them. On the windowless wall across from him gaped two fireplaces, on the left and on the right, and each bore a tin tub for prisoners to piss in.

Judge Parker's court would soon be in session and the stench of urine wouldn't only rise up the chimneys to the outdoors and attract slugs and gnats. Bass knew from years of experience that it would hotly seep between the ceiling planks and the courtroom flooring so that by midday the soles of your boots would smell of it if you sat for long on the witness stand.

Four-sided timbers held up the ceiling seven feet from the damp flagstone floor, and the four dusty Creeks Bass had brought in from Tishomingo last week congregated around the pillar closest to him. Without speaking, they stood and stared in facing pairs—east and west, north and south—as if the pillar were a maypole made of rough water instead of planed hardwood and as soon as it stopped rippling and clearly reflected what each most needed to find, they would strike up their dance.

Chub Moore was the quiet, simmering sort who appeared to watch the Creeks, too, from where he leaned nearby, against the gated lawyer box, as if he expected to be a priority to his court-appointed attorney this Monday morning. He was Chickasaw in height, but there was a way about him that seemed to account for all races, with his copper-colored skin and wavy, wiry hair and broad nose and high cheekbones and narrow eyes and lips like a minnow.

"Hell!" a prisoner shouted, and Bass turned away from Chub Moore to see what the commotion was about at the other end of the cell.

"Simmer," a second prisoner grumbled, also faceless. A few others stretched their arms or legs, but the prisoners by and large remained curled and shrouded in shadows on the floor and ignored the interruption.

"You know, Hell on the Border's what they call this godforsaken place. You heard that, right?" the first prisoner said, projecting louder now and his voice rang against the walls.

"Shit, like we ain't heard," the other prisoner answered from the dark middle of the room. His speech seemed muffled as if he held a hand over his mouth.

"There's another cell just like this one next to us," the first prisoner continued. "Just like it, can you believe the godforsaken luck of that shit? Jesus, can you think of anything worse than two places just as bad?"

A bear body rose from the dark middle, and the thin window light exposed the outline of a beard that doubled the width of his head. "Close up your mouth hole," he said. His beard raked every word. "We need no talkers here. Talk's what brung us here. Think back to when you was just about to turn," he said, pointing a short but stout arm at the other prisoner shape, "and you'll see talk is the actual fucking source of how your life suddenly soured to shit. Hell on the Border? People say lots of things. You think this bad? You ain't lived bad. I suggest you simmer. I'm telling you, simmer."

Bass watched the bearded man lower back into the shadows, and that's when one of the Creeks, shirtless and glinting as if from an inner light, charged with flying braids toward the pillar and rammed it with his shoulder.

Those nearby on the floor scrambled to back away, and a second Creek charged, letting out a fierce grunt as his shoulder bounced off the solid timber.

"What the hell?" the bearded one said, raking his words.

A third Creek charged the pillar, and then the last one took his turn. They heaved breaths and winced in despair at the immoveable pillar.

Bass braced himself against the limestone and stood up. "You Creeks ain't gonna bring the courthouse down," he said, even though he knew the Creeks didn't speak enough English to understand him. His boots rasped against the flagstone floor as he stepped toward them, speaking in Creek, urging them to sit and be calm, and gradually they did. "This ain't the way to wipe a place like this out." He was speaking now to everyone but the Creeks.

The cell fell silent as faces turned as if leaves after a rain.

"You wanna strap horse hooves on your shoulders so you can battle-ram this place to the ground and flee free of it?" Bass asked. "You do right. That's it. No need to talk, it's true, unless you talking to God or talking of him so others will do right right along with you. That's it."

The gate of the lawyer box rattled, and Bass spun around. Chub Moore was racing ghostlike toward him, leading with his head and growling. Bass squared down, ready to throw him off, but Chub charged past him and the crown of his head struck the Creeks' pillar, not on a flat side but on one of the corners, and the sound of the meeting was the wet crack of a watermelon.

Chub wobbled left and right, his feet danced, and then, as slowly as a tree, he fell backward onto the floor.

Bass hopped to him and touched his fingertips to Chub's dark head, his sticky hair, the rough cleaved mark up and down his crown, the swelling already fruitlike around it.

"Two places just as bad," the prisoner said from the other side of the cell. "Can you believe the godforsaken luck?"

Bass wiped his hand on his trousers and dragged Chub by the shoulders to his corner and set his head on his coat. He called outside for the turnkeys to fetch Doc Semmes, and for the next hour Bass sat with Chub, pressing a coat sleeve against his head to stop the bleeding.

He wondered if laundry hung on a rope strung between the sticks on the old plantation in Texas—white squares like these windows where slaves like Bass were once strung for punishment. Or perhaps a cow in calf was tied there today. Occasionally, Chub moaned like a cow several pastures away. Honest as a cow, saying, *Here I am, don't follow me, but here I am.*

He wondered if Jennie, her black limbs on white linen, was lying awake and fretting about him being away yet again and not knowing yet again for how long. He could see her side of the bed, the left side, sinking deeper and deeper.

Doc Semmes would be rising from his own bed by now, away from his own wife, to dress and eat and sip coffee from a saucer the way he always drank his coffee. Perhaps after riding his horse through the morning, he'd tie his horse to the same post Theodore Barnes tied his, and they would walk to the jail together, to this side, the left side, first.

Theodore Barnes had the reputation of being the best attorney money could buy. If he'd ever lost a case, nobody in Fort Smith thought to talk about it.

◆ ◆ ◆

Chub Moore's cow gradually wandered too far away to be heard, and soundlessly he stopped breathing. When Doc Semmes arrived, he verified that Chub was dead, and two guards carried out his corpse.

While the door stood open, Bass heard his name popping up like mushrooms across the yard.

The day guards relieved the night guards and Bass answered the question everyone peeked his head in to ask. "I did," he said to this guard, that deputy, "but didn't mean to."

Half past nine, the outer door to the lawyer box opened once more and into the flood of light walked Lester, holding a key out in front of him, and Theodore Barnes followed, wearing a striped three-piece suit and spectacles and holding an unlit cigar.

Bass realized he'd been holding his breath. He let it out and stood up.

"Bass," Lester called through the bars as he unlocked the gate.

Bass stepped over outstretched legs and wove between the Creeks. He thanked the Good Lord and nodded to Lester. He entered the box with his hand out to Theodore.

"Would expect anybody but you," Theodore said.

They vigorously pumped each other's hand as Lester clanged the gate shut.

"Appreciate you coming," Bass said. He was thirsty and swallowed to keep from coughing.

Lester shuffled past them and swept the light back outside as he shut the outer door and turned the lock.

Theodore retreated until the heels of his shoes bumped the door, and Bass stepped in close.

"I talked to Sonny already," Theodore said in a lowered voice, "but I want to hear it from you, from the beginning, and I mean leave none out." He tucked his cigar in his mouth, and as Bass began, Theodore began to roll the cigar in place with his tongue and teeth, as if to keep time while he lost time listening.

Bass didn't want to leave none out. He began where he thought it began, with the stray bull pup begging, and spoke long past the last time a prisoner moseyed up to the box for any excuse to try to overhear. He spoke until Theodore's soaked cigar looked like a log turning in an eddy of a river. Bass ended with old man Nat, how Bass had tracked him down and waited for him and led him to camp to inspect, too late, Willy's wound.

Bass took a half-step back to see Theodore's eyes, brown but black in the jail. Theodore looked out into the cell and nodded, still rolling the cigar. He removed it from his mouth. "Bass," he said, shifting his eyes to Bass's eyes now, "you want to tell the truth, I know you."

Bass nodded. "I'll be laying my hand on the Bible."

"You know sometimes truth in the court of law doesn't sound much like itself. I know you know that. I know you know sometimes it sounds a whole lot worse than a lie, and a lie can sound so much sweeter and really be what is true."

"You know me to tell the truth."

Theodore stilled his cigar and produced a match from his coat pocket. "I do."

"Everybody do," Bass said, watching him turn to the nearest wall and strike the match off a stone.

"No, Bass," Theodore said, "everybody *did.*" He stoked the cigar, rotating it. He breathed smoke. "By the time we go to trial, they will forget what they ever thought about you. I've seen it happen."

Bass didn't know what to say so he listened. If he didn't like what he heard, he could always hire Lewis Clayton or Edward Marcum instead. They were good lawyers, too.

"I want you to consider something," Theodore said. "Are you listening?"

Bass shifted his weight. "I'm listening."

Theodore leaned in. "What if Willy didn't kill the pup? What if you did?" He leaned back and his eyebrows shrugged above the wire of his spectacles.

Bass lowered his eyes to the glass of the spectacles and the smudges he couldn't imagine having to see through. "Help me out, Theo. You seemed to heard a different story from the one I just told."

Theodore slid his cigar from his mouth and leaned in again. "If you killed the pup, you lose your motive to kill Willy, see? We have to take your motive away."

Bass crossed his arms and through his shirt sleeves felt the rough skin of his elbows. "But I wouldn't'a done that. That ain't how it ever woulda happened."

"Bass, you did right to go after a doctor. You did all you could do. If you wanted him to die, you wouldn't have gone to that trouble and that expense. Of course, you didn't mean to kill him. Hell, you didn't even mean to shoot him. You were cleaning your rifle is all, right? That's what your man Floyd attests."

"I told you," Bass said, his whisper a deep one, "I meant to nick him, to back him down."

"But pulling the trigger on purpose is all the jury will hear. Is that the truth you want them to hear? That you meant to kill your Negro?"

"My cook."

Theodore tapped Bass on the chest, his cigar between his fingers, the smoke rising. "Let's not leave it to the jury to decide how to see it."

Bass lowered his face and shut his eyes and held them shut. He prayed the jury of white men would recognize the truth when they heard it.

"You've got a lot to think about," Theodore said. "Your testimony will carry you north or will carry you south."

Murmurs grew beyond the outer door and keys clanked. Bass opened his eyes and the lock turned.

He and Theodore shuffled away from the door as it opened but only wide enough for Lester to insert his head of wispy hair.

"Can we have a few minutes more?" Theodore asked.

Lester regarded only Bass. "Somebody else here to see you." He pushed the door wide and stepped back, and a man with gray hair and black clothes absorbed the light. The man ducked his head as he stepped across the threshold with a hat he held to his chest.

Bass stiffened his posture, his spirit buoyed by Judge Parker's unexpected presence, an intercession he dared not pray for. Not until the form stood completely in the jail cell in front of him, against the backdrop of a near-wintry glare, did the man's thinner frame reveal itself, did he raise his sallow face, his tiny dark eyes, his spearhead of gray whiskers.

"Ole Bass," he smirked, exposing yellowed teeth.

Bass gazed unflinchingly back but couldn't speak, or didn't think to. No words came.

"He's got representation already," Theodore told the visitor.

"Tell him who I am, Ole Bass."

Bass pealed apart his dry lips. "I'll leave you to tell him," he said, calm but his breathing coming faster.

His old master, the last one but now as old as Bass remembered the first one, turned to Theodore. "I am George Robertson Reeves, and though I represent, too, I represent only in the Lone Star State of Texas. And as speaker of the House, it's a principle of mine to represent only our upstanding citizens. No riffraff. So trust me, sir, the edge of the world is all yours."

Theodore crinkled his eyes at Bass, who looked only blankly. He hitched his pants and regarded George Reeves again. "What's your business?"

George Reeves set his Stetson on his head, as if he were preparing to leave, or simply wished to present himself taller. The crown purpled where it folded with a deep crease, and a gold band pin shone on the right. "I rode a long way over night to speak to Ole Bass a moment, if you and Ole Bass will consent to it. You should know we were once bosom friends, my own inseparable twin brother. For better or worse, we two, for the time, were wedded, were family, Ole Bass and me, back in the good ole days, were we not?" He looked away from Theodore and Theodore looked away from him to look at Bass together.

"Families don't buy or sell or give each other away," Bass said. "They don't burn their spirit on a spit."

"The best families aren't perfect, but they nevertheless protect each other," George Reeves said. "They feed and clothe each other."

"And they don't cheat and humiliate each other."

George Reeves laughed. "They do, boy, frequently."

"Yours do."

"So," George Reeves said, weaving his hands prayerlike, "you wouldn't attack your family and steal their property? You arrest horse thieves, don't you? And murderers of lawmen and innocent children? I mean, well, you used to do a lot of things."

"What purpose do you have here?" Theodore asked him.

Without regarding Theodore, George Reeves craned his neck toward Bass to press his smile upon him. "I find you in a tight spot, a familiar spot. You must be ashamed of your actions. Feel cheated and humiliated more than ever, true? Well, that's why I've come.

Because families should grow closer in times like these. At some point, after a dispute, they should right wrongs. Will you grant me that opportunity today, Ole Bass? Will you give me a moment, just us, to talk?"

"I ain't Ole Bass to you, George."

George Reeves laughed. He turned to Theodore and Lester. "*Bass*, then. I won't squabble."

Theodore placed a hand on Bass's back. "Your decision."

Bass eyed his former master, remembering him as taller, with or without his hat. He balled his face-busters and turned to Theodore and Lester. "Y'all leave us cause I got things to say myself."

"Make it quick," Lester said. "We got water rounds in a bit." He heaved the outer door open.

"I'll wait around," Theodore told Bass before stepping out. Lester followed and locked the door.

George Reeves shifted to the other side of the lawyer box and grinned at Bass from a greater distance. "All that running and you're right back at the beginning, here with me."

"I ain't here to stay," Bass said. "Didn't kill you when I had every chance, and now, look at you, you begging to give me another go. But I ain't no murderer."

"If only your granddaddy were here at my side to see you. You'd be such a disappointment."

Bass laughed at George Reeves's grin, a childish grin, as he stood there before the shadows of the jail as if at the mouth of a cave he'd just about come out of. "Ole Bass," said Bass, "let me tell you about Ole Bass. He'd grin that same n—— grin you grinning now if he was here at your side and I was to choke you out, I know that. But I ain't no murderer no matter what you or him want. I'm a U.S. deputy marshal and not bad at it, glory to God, not bad, and I know you heard because you here."

George Reeves continued to show his yellowed teeth. His black hat, hardly visible in the shadows, a grackle with its wings spread, appeared to nest on the wrinkles of his forehead. "I came to thank you, Bass," he said. "That's why I've come. You've been giving n——s hope for a long time, but now you're giving me hope. You're giving a lot of people hope. *People*, Bass, I'm talking about people." He took a step closer. "If you can't be trusted to uphold the law—*you*, Bass Reeves, perhaps the best at being not bad a n—— has ever been— then which of your kind can be?" He took another step, bridging the distance. "Thanks to you, we could have a legitimate basis to repeal the Thirteenth Amendment. A ratifying convention is in motion in Texas as we speak, and other states will be watching. You, Bass, might just help bring slavery back."

Bass flexed his fists down by his sides and stepped forward to meet him. "I ain't gonna redeem you. Not this soothing savage. You keep your splintered heart in your wolfish world. You came here to hunt whales? Well, good. Get ready."

The old master showed surprise in his eyes, and then delight. "You learned to read?"

"Didn't have to. Your wife taught my wife how, remember? She can read to me fine. *Moby-Dick*, sure, but I'm partial to *Uncle Tom's Cabin*."

"So, I do leave a white and turbid wake wherever I sail," the old master said, grinning again. "We are family, aren't we, Bass? You never forgot the things I taught you. You never forgot *me*." He unclasped his hands and reached out for an embrace.

Bass jumped back and swung his arms out in a rage, striking the bars. He raised his face as if to bite the planks. "Lester!" He struck the bars again. "Lester!"

George Reeves laughed and the lock turned and the sun spilled in instant heat.

Bass panted. His lungs burned and fists ached to keep striking. "Get him outta here."

Lester motioned for George Reeves to move on. "Long enough," he said.

George Reeves paused to tip his hat. "I enjoyed our reunion."

Bass refused to blink or look away. His thoughts reeled. The old master's eyes were just eyes.

"I'll see you at the hanging," George Reeves said. His leather shoes trailed out, and the sun hid as if behind a passing cloud.

Bass eyed Lester. "Fetch Theodore," he said, and he lowered his eyes to focus on the flagstones and the muddy imprints of boots and shoes and on what to do.

"That'll be it for today, though." Lester turned about and waved for Theodore. "Come on but make it quick. Past water time."

Theodore returned and his shoes rasped the floor. "Well, Bass?"

Lester left but without shutting the outer door behind him. The floor went murky as Theodore approached, slowly, as if wading. Bass lifted his face to receive him. Theo, without his cigar, looked milder, meeker, lost without his prop.

"Need you to do one thing," Bass said.

"Of course." Theodore stepped closer.

"Talk to Clayton and Marcum for me."

"What? Hiring them instead of me?"

Bass shook his head. "I still want you, but I want them hitched to us, too. We won't leave the court one good lawyer. How's that? Fact, let's hire up everybody. The good and the bad. The Lord made me rich for something. This must be it."

Theodore smiled from the eyes as if they shared much more history than they did, or as if they were right this moment becoming bosom friends, inseparable twin brothers, which made Bass miss Strawberry, the one forever waiting for him beneath a tree at the border, whisking his tail.

Lester and another turnkey swayed into the doorway with a water barrel sloshing between them. They grunted as they set it down just inside the lawyer box.

Bass gripped Theodore's shoulders and gazed through the hazy glass of his spectacles and into his enlarged eyes. "Willy can just be mad I killed the pup and didn't let him." He smiled into his mustache, then had to swallow.

Acknowledgments

The author expresses his gratitude to these invaluable sources of information and inspiration: *Black Gun, Silver Star: The Life and Legend of Frontier Marshal Bass Reeves* by Art T. Burton, *Storm and Stampede on the Chisholm* by Hubert E. Collins, *Hell on the Border* by S. W. Harman, *Africans and Seminoles: From Removal to Emancipation* by Daniel F. Littlefield Jr., and *The Legend of Bass Reeves* by Gary Paulsen. And to the top-shelf staff at the University of Nebraska Press, thanks again for all that you continue to do!